BACKSTABBER!

If I hadn't turned when I did, that long knife would have slid in right next to my spine, just above the heart. As it was, I took it in the left shoulder, straight in under the main muscle and out through the skin above my shoulder blade.

My whole arm seared with the pain of it, then just went numb and dead on me, and I felt the tingle of shock going up my neck. I was turning when it hit, and instinct made me spin right on around. As I did, the wrench of my twist pulled the knife out of his hand.

He laughed, and I looked right into the grinning face of Joshua Sutton. Another man was beside him. Just past them in the shadows was somebody else. Joshua grinned at me like he was the cat and I was the mouse, and stepped back. The fellow beside him went for a sidearm and it seemed like I was frozen, like we were at the bottom of a molasses jug, and I was watching his hand go down for that gun. . . .

MORE OF THE HOTTEST WESTERNS!

GUNN #18: THE GOLDEN LADY (1298, $2.25)
by Jory Sherman

Gunn's got a beautiful miner's daughter in front of him, and hard-case killers closing in on him from the rear. It looks like he'll be shooting in all directions!

GUNN #19: HIGH MOUNTAIN HUSSY (1348, $2.25)
by Jory Sherman

Gunn gets intimate with a dark-haired temptress—and she's revealing it all! Her father's been murdered, but not before writing a cryptic message that Gunn's obliged to decipher—before a killer deciphers Gunn!

GUNN #20: TEN-GALLON TEASE (1378, $2.25)
by Jory Sherman

With Apache raiders and a desperate outlaw gang each planning an ambush, Gunn's chance to make fast money selling California horses to the U.S. Cavalry looks slim. He's lucky he can count on the services of a wild and beautiful tomboy to help him in the clinches!

SHELTER #18: TABOO TERRITORY (1379, $2.25)
by Paul Ledd

A ruthless death-battalion member is Shelter's target—but Shelter's got to get the Baja to take his shot. And with the help of a dark-haired Baja beauty, he may just succeed!

SHELTER #19: THE HARD MEN (1428, $2.25)
by Paul Ledd

Shelter's aiming to cross another member of the death battalion off his hit list—except he's hunting the wrong man. Morgan's in for trouble, and it takes the hot touch of an eager squaw to get him ready for action!

SHELTER #20: SADDLE TRAMP (1464, $2.25)
by Paul Ledd

Tracking another killer, Shelter takes on the identity of a murdered U.S. marshal and lays down the law. And a buxom bargirl named Lola likes the way the law lays!

Available wherever paperbacks are sold, or order direct from the Publisher. Send cover price plus 50¢ per copy for mailing and handling to Zebra Books, 475 Park Avenue South, New York, N.Y. 10016. DO NOT SEND CASH.

GUNPOWDER GLORY

By Dan Parkinson

ZEBRA BOOKS
KENSINGTON PUBLISHING CORP.

ZEBRA BOOKS

are published by

Kensington Publishing Corp.
475 Park Avenue South
New York, N.Y. 10016

Copyright © 1984 by Dan Parkinson

All rights reserved. No part of this book may be reproduced in any form or by any means without the prior written consent of the Publisher, excepting brief quotes used in reviews.

First printing: September, 1984

Printed in the United States of America

CHAPTER ONE

It was short of a season since the plague had burned itself out in the Sugar Creek country, and there wasn't much doing. For a fact, there weren't many left right then to do. There never had been a lot of folks in those parts. It was a country still more wild than not. And now there was hardly a family in the hills that wasn't mourning someone lost to the fever.

Those of us who hadn't come down were mostly just tending our affairs, staying far apart and solitary. It can be like that at the downhill end of hard times. Folks need a time of peace, to remember their dead and pick up their lives, and they need to run shy of one another for a while. We went into Burnham when we had to and stayed just long enough to swap for supplies, and mostly whoever else was there kept to his own ground and we kept to ours. It was always the way of the land not to be overly neighborly, and the fever had emphasized the custom.

By and large they were good folks around there, solid and honest. Most would come to your aid when you needed them and let you alone the rest of the time. Indiana never was a socializing land anyhow, and the circumstances behind a lot of the folks' coming to those Sugar Creek hills made it even more a private place. There were prayer meetings and barn raisings now and again, or had been, but that fever had hung a heavy pall over the hills and it would be a time before folks eased up.

In Burnham most of the burned buildings had been cleared away and there were two or three new cabins now, so the bad times weren't as visible. But there was sign aplenty up on the hill, at the graveyard. A lot of new sod had been turned there in those black months. The little new mounds without headstones outnumbered the old grassed-over graves that were marked.

That graveyard was where I began my journey on a cold, late-winter day.

At our place there were five of us left: Pa and the girls, my big brother Harley, and me. Ma was gone, resting now on the hillside at Burnham with little Thelma and my oldest brother, Willard, and his bride. Ma and Mary Ann were taken early, then Willard went out of his head and ran off somewhere and we found him two days later floating at a gravel bank on Sugar Creek. When we carried him up to bury him alongside Mary Ann, near Ma's grave, there were other families up there, too, doing their own burying. And later when little Thelma was gone and we took her there, there were others at the graveyard then, too.

It hit Pa fearful hard when Ma was gone, and he just couldn't handle it when more of his family followed her. I know it hurt me about as bad seeing him just fall in on himself and turn old and feeble all of a sudden, as it did to lose the others. Where there had been that strapping man that I'd loved and admired— the selfsame man that had been taken all the way back to New York City that time to have his name read off on a roll of honor and that had been handed a new Colt's revolving gun personally by Colonel Colt— where that man had been, now there was a haunted old man as innocent as a baby, and I still loved him just as much, or maybe more.

As that winter set in he mostly sat by the fire, wrapped up in his shawl, but now and again he'd put on his coat and hat and one of us would walk with him into Burnham so he could climb that hill and kneel there and talk things over with Ma. She was always the level-headed one, and now that she was gone he still looked to her. I don't believe he really saw she was gone. He just knew that now he had to make that long walk whenever he got to missing her.

The thing about that fever was that it left some folks dead and gone, and others alive and lost. And it left a few, like Joey Sutton, twisted in the head.

Most of the Suttons never had been of much account, even though they were shirttail kin of ours, Ma having been a Sutton and second cousin to old Abe Sutton, Joey's pa. There was a history of bad blood between our families, the Suttons and the Burkes, that went a ways back to the redlands of Kentucky. The old hostilities had eased off some after Ma married Pa, but I always had the feeling that given the chance some of the Suttons might just start up again. Old Abe would be a man to remember long-gone grudges, and that Joshua, he just cottoned to trouble.

Their place was over the hill from ours, down by Rock Run. I had grown up around the Sutton boys, but there was never a good feeling among us. I got on well enough with Aaron; we were of an age and he was decent enough, but that Joshua was a wild and spooky one. I never could take to him, nor could many others. Being around him was like being in a dark room with a bad dog. There just wasn't any telling what he was like to do next.

Isaac was the oldest of old Abe's tribe, about the age of my brother Harley. Then there was Joshua, then Aaron, who was my age, then young Abraham, that everybody called Sonny, then the twins, Joey and Jenny. Old Abe's score at siring sons was perfect right up to that last round. Little Jenny was the wild card in the Sutton progeny, and as the years went by she came up pure tomboy, trying to keep up with all those brothers.

They had been without a mother since the twins were babies and their place showed it. Jenny managed to brighten things up a bit as she got older, but old Abe was no help to her, and the only ones turned a hand to keeping up the farm were Isaac and Aaron, with Sonny helping out now and again when it suited him. Joshua spent his time running the woods or looking for trouble, and Joey was usually off skylarking.

They lost kin in the plague, too. Isaac took down and died in a few days. Then Joey caught it, and it hit him hard but he didn't die. He lived, but it left him wrong in the head.

There were others like him around the country, some peaceable enough, but others running loose in the backwoods wild as hydrophoby dogs, so most of us took to carrying weapons when we were out and around, just in case.

I always had a special knack with a handgun—Pa had joked me about "pistol-witching," but the way he said it he was more puzzled than amused—so when my brother Harley favored carrying the rifle, I began strapping on Pa's fine old Walker revolver that he got from Colonel Colt, and wearing it when I was out.

There had already been one place shot up by a daft. Nobody was hurt but they could have been. It was a time to keep your protection close to hand.

It was on a grey, cold day with snow threatening when Pa got the miseries again and decided he would go talk to Ma about it. So he bundled up and set out down the road, and when I looked up from chopping wood and saw that hunched old man plodding away, I decided to go along to keep him company. I got my gun and put on my heavy coat, and when I caught him at the top of the hill I fell in alongside. When we passed the Suttons' north pasture old Abe and Joshua were out there. They had their dun mule hitched to a load of cordwood and had got it bogged down in a seep. Abe Sutton was cutting at the mule with a switch, hollering and getting red in the face.

Joshua was leaning up against a tree, grinning in that way of his as he watched the show. The poor old mule was heaving for all it was worth, lathered and starting to foam. The sight was enough to make a man sick. I kept my mouth shut and we passed by, but even so old Abe spied us and yelled, "What the devil are you starin' at, Jeremy Burke? You mind your own damned business!" Then he took another cut at that poor mule.

Joshua just stood there by that tree and grinned. He had that Pennsylvania rifle of his across his arm. As we went on by I was holding my jaws clamped tight and my shoulders hard. Pa said, in that quiet way of his, "Ease up, boy. It's the way of the world and you can't change it all at once."

In town we walked along the slushy street where the mud had thawed and was freezing over again on top, and turned right at the path up the hill. I heard some kind of ruckus going on down the street, but didn't pay it any mind.

When we came up to Ma's grave Pa took off his

hat and knelt down there on the cold ground. I knew he wanted some privacy so I wandered around looking at the names, and those sad little mounds that didn't have names on them yet. It was right then that all hell broke loose.

There was shouting down the hill and a woman screamed, then there was a gunshot. When I turned around young Joey Sutton was running up the hill toward us, shouting and giggling, waving a repeating rifle around over his head. Down on the street behind him a man was crawling up on Henley's boardwalk, dragging a bloody leg.

About the time I saw Joey he saw Pa kneeling there by Ma's grave, and he just stopped, brought that rifle down, and shot him.

Just like that. No warning, no reason, no sense to it at all. He just saw the old man's stooped back and put a bullet in it, then cocked the rifle again and swung it toward me.

I was standing there empty-handed. But somehow, even while that rifle muzzle was swinging around, I came up with the Walker gun in my hand and it was spitting fire and thunder and I didn't miss. Joey Sutton never got the chance to squeeze that trigger again. He just went limp and sagged. I heard him fall just as I reached Pa, and Pa was just slumping over. It had all happened that fast. I got an arm around him and turned him over so I could see his face. He shuddered and sighed, and those old grey eyes opened.

"Who shot me, boy?"

"It was Joey Sutton, Pa. He just ran up and fired . . . I shot him, Pa. He's dead."

"Little Joey Sutton," he whispered. Then he looked me in the eye and he said, "Don't blame Joey, boy. He ain't right in the head. You just leave him be, now."

"But I killed him, Pa. I shot him down!"

He didn't hear me. He just looked past me, like he was seeing a sight he'd never seen before, and said kind of offhand, "Your Ma is a Sutton, boy, and she's the finest thing that bunch ever come up with. Don't ever shoot a Sutton, Jeremy. You hear me?"

"I hear you, Pa."

Then he looked for a moment like he'd come wide awake and worried, and he tried to raise his head closer to me.

"Pledge to me, boy. Promise me, you'll never shoot a Sutton." His face was white as new snow, but the eyes in it were demanding, pleading.

"I promise, Pa. I pledge."

That eased him. He lay back on my arm, a deep shudder went through him and he coughed up some blood, and his eyes opened wide.

"Martha!" he choked. "Martha, give me your hand. I can't see!"

By the time I'd blinked the hot tears out of my eyes he was gone. After a while I laid him down gently, there on Ma's grave. There were people all around now, but I couldn't see them very well.

When we buried Pa the next morning, right there next to Ma, the Suttons were over across the way putting Joey in the ground. I wanted to go over and tell them I was sorry about it all, but the look on old Abe's face—and on Joshua's when he looked around—said there was no good to be done by it.

After the preacher had gone along and I was standing there with Harley and the girls, all of us trying to think of a comfort for one another, Aaron Sutton came over and took off his hat and stood with us a minute, looking down at Pa's resting place. Sonny and Joshua had followed him part way over but hung back from coming right up to us. Joshua had his rifle in his hands and he looked oddly excited, anticipating.

Aaron finished his respects and put his hat on.

"Jeremy," he said, "I don't like what's happened, not one bit, but there's something you need to know. Our pa's firm in his mind that you are to blame. I expect he'll land on me for even talking to you now, but it's only right you should know."

He expected me to say something, but I just waited.

"I mean it, Jeremy. I don't know what's going to happen, but my pa aims to see you dead."

"Are you coming for me, Aaron?" I kept my voice just as level as pond ice, and he dropped his eyes.

"I don't want to, Jeremy, I surely don't. But I can't speak for Joshua, you know that." He turned and looked toward his brothers. "And nobody speaks for Sonny."

"Then what would you have me do?"

He fixed his eyes on his boots and kept them there. "Go away, Jeremy," he said. "We've talked about the West, you and me. Go on and see what's out there. Go now." When he looked up he looked almost desperate. "There's been enough trouble here."

Harley and the girls had come up beside me. Harley looked ready to fight all three of them if need be, but Aaron Sutton just looked at all of us, one after another, and there was a sadness in him.

"Talk to him, Harley," he said. "If he stays here there will be killing, and there's no need of more."

"I wish it didn't have to come to this," I told him. "We've been friends, Aaron."

"Yeah." He was looking at his boots again. "But I can only answer for myself."

For a minute or two then we all just stood there, and I had a wary eye on the other Sutton boys in the background. Joshua was grinning and fidgeting with his rifle. Sonny just stared away into the distance. My coat was pushed back and Aaron's gaze kept returning to the darkwood butt of the Walker hanging at my belt. I knew a little how he felt. He was concerned about me to a proper point. But we had done some shooting together in better days and now he was worried about his brothers even more.

He straightened up then and stepped back. "I'll say it like this, Jeremy. I have nothing against you for Joey's being dead. I understand you had to. But Joshua don't feel like I do, and I don't know how Sonny feels about it. I guess if I was to lose another brother to you, Jeremy, I'd have to change my mind, no matter what the circumstances. You think on it, Jeremy, and think soon."

He walked away with his back straight as a door pole and the other two fell in beside him—Joshua tossing another of those wicked grins back at me—and they headed down the hill to where old Abe sat his rig at the roadside. Jenny was there, too, and she looked worried.

We didn't talk on the way home. When we got to the house Mildred set about making a meal, Harley stirred up the fire in the hearth, and little Margie went to rummaging around in pantry shelves and bins. I sat down by the window. I had some deciding to do.

Go west, Aaron Sutton had told me. I was of two minds about it. One part of me raised its hackles and bared its teeth at the very thought of running away. Stay and face it out, it said. Fight them if that's what they want.

As a matter of fact, I wasn't worried about my hide. I never grew up in a velvet box. I knew what I could do, and I didn't believe the whole Sutton tribe could take me out if I set my mind against it. I had been in more than one ruckus down to the meeting hall, and I also had that witches' touch with a handgun that had been with me since the first day I ever lifted one. I took no great pride in that—Pa wouldn't have seen a natural skill as a prideful thing—but I knew what I could do, if I had to.

I had no real fear of Joshua Sutton, for one. Mean as a snake he might be, mean clear through, but he had no real substance and he wasn't very smart—although he was convinced that nobody was nearly as clever as he. Joshua was wild and mean, and had a cruel streak like none I had seen before, but he wasn't a real source of concern.

I would worry a whole lot more about Aaron if it came to that. We had been passing friends off and on, and I knew him. Aaron Sutton was a man to do what he decided needed doing, and once begun, nothing stood in his way. Aaron was solid, methodical, and determined when he made up his mind. He could be deadly.

About Sonny Sutton, young Abraham, there was little to know. Sonny was a mystery to everyone. He lived within himself and turned a blank face to the world. There might be a lot behind that face, but only he knew. I had known Sonny since we were shirttail tads and I had seldom come close to understanding him.

The first inner voice told me, stay. See it through. But there was another. A few years ago, when I was twenty or so, I probably would not have ever heard this second one. Look around you, it said. Ma and

Pa are gone, and Willard and Mary Ann, and little Thelma. Now there are just these to care for. There's Harley, big and serious, twenty-nine years old and still unmarried, although by the light in Maxine Studer's eyes she may remedy that soon enough. There's quiet Mildred, sweet and still, always helping out, waiting for the day her beau will come back from the gold fields and take her away on a great white horse. And there's little Margie, sweet, feisty, sharp-tongued and soft-hearted Margie. Whoever gets her to wife will be luckier than he might ever know.

Look at them, the voice inside me said. When the shooting starts, which of them will fall before you get it stopped?

And there was another voice, old and quiet but deep in my mind, that said, promise me, boy, don't ever shoot a Sutton.

I was listening to them all, those inner voices, when suddenly I noticed what Margie was doing at the pantry. She had got out the big old buffalo gun we kept there and was rummaging around for ball to fit it. There was no doubt at all on her face. She was fixing to help me fight the Suttons.

That made up my mind for me. I stood up, went to the kitchen table, and they gathered around.

"I'm going away," I told them. "I want to see what it looks like out west."

My mind was made up and I didn't let them argue. I told them of my promise to Pa, as he lay there on Ma's grave with a bullet in him. I would not fight the Suttons, not if I could help it.

They thought it over, and Harley nodded. "Take the Morgan, Jeremy. He's the fastest thing around. He'll get you where you're going and back."

Mildred and Margie were both crying, but they

didn't argue, bless them. They understood. After supper Harley and I cast up a sack full of .44 balls for the Walker, while Mildred fussed around rolling blankets, packing things I might need and generally fretting herself into feeling better. Margie got down Ma's old cookie jar and brought me the money from it. There was about four hundred dollars there. I kept fifty and put the rest back. They'd need seed money come spring, and I wanted Mildred to have a wedding dress when her beau came back from the gold fields.

I went out with Harley to saddle the Morgan by lantern light, then went in once more to tell my sisters good-bye. They were bawling again, but they kissed me and wished me safe journey. One final handclasp from Harley, and I mounted up and headed out.

It was dark and a light snow was falling. It was thirty miles to the Illinois line, and I would be there by morning.

CHAPTER TWO

The Morgan made good time along the dark road. From our place to the Wabash he knew the road as well as I did, and he didn't need light to find his way. Snow was falling steadily now, a constant brush of cold feathers on my face and hands. When we passed a farmhouse near the road where the lamps were burning late, their glow showed the earth turning white with winter's blanket.

I had no particular place in mind. I would just head west and see where I turned up. There was a longing in me at leaving home, at knowing that all that's dear was back there getting further away by the mile. But matching that was an excitement, the primal itch to go west, to see the other side of the hill. It is something in the blood of the Burkes, I think. When the first one over—my great-grandfather—landed on American soil with a young wife and two little kids, he set foot on the good ground and put the other foot in front of it and didn't stop until he was past the settlements. There in the wilds of Pennsylvania he cleared his ground, built his cabin, and planted his crops.

Then my grandpa, when he came of age, went on west to settle in Ohio, then moved again down into Kentucky. And Pa, after his time in the fighting in Texas, when he had helped save a troop of militia and been cited for bravery and honor—that was why he was called up to New York City later and presented with that brand new Walker Colt—had come back to Kentucky, seen how things were building up, and packed us up and moved to western Indiana.

Now Pa was gone to be with Ma, and I was going west. I had some things going for me, including a good horse and a fine gun.

That big pistol at my side was, in full name, a Whitneyville Walker. It was designed by Colonel Colt, built by the Eli Whitney Company, and named for Captain Walker. It was a big handgun. Pa had practiced a little with it, and I had practiced a lot. I had a skill with it, right enough.

It rode in a holster that I had made by tacking wet hide around the gun, letting it dry on a board, then lacing the shaped hide at the back. The finished, oiled sheath was a glove fit for the big gun, and it could come out of there and into hand in an instant. Pa had watched me with it time and again, and he had told me always to be sure I was in charge of it, and not the other way around.

The big Walker hung now at my hip and its comfortable weight was what I had left of Pa as I passed the Veedersburg road and left my home county in the dark of night.

Riding alone at night through western Indiana was never considered good practice. Those wooded hills are a lonesome place at best, harboring a mixed bag of folks not recommended for encounter. Some of them are just poor people taken to road agentry to buy their bread, and some are plain outlaws. Of the two, the poor people are the most dangerous. Their guns generally aren't in good shape, and they tend to be nervous when robbing. More than one traveler through those lonesome hills has died of no hard feelings.

But on that snowy night there wasn't anybody skulking around. With the first chill light of dawn I came down to the bank of the Wabash and chucked some rocks across at the shack on the other side to wake up the ferryman. When I saw light in the window over there I unsaddled the Morgan, rubbed him down and tossed a blanket over him, then hung the feedbag strap over his ears and waited for the ferry.

He came across in his own good time, cranky and griping about people traveling at ungodly hours, and I led the horse aboard and we started back across. The river was high and swelling, with ice skim crackling along its banks. Winter never gives up easy in that part of the country.

We were near the west dock when a gunshot sounded across the water and something whipped past my face. By pure reflex the big gun was in my hand by the time I got my head turned, and I was looking down the barrel at a man on a horse, back on the river bank I had just left. It was Joshua Sutton, hat down over his ears, greatcoat turned high on his shoulders, smoke curling from his rifle. I hadn't expected him, at least not so soon. I had thought Aaron might hold his brothers in check for a little while at least. But this one must have been no more than a mile behind me when I left the house.

Joshua had fired and missed, and he would have reloading to do. So I holstered the Walker, got the ferryman out from behind the cable winch, and helped him heave the barge in to the dock. Then I asked him what his winch handle was worth and he just goggled at me and went back to whining and griping.

"Would a dollar cover it?" I demanded, and he

nodded.

There was an old rusty axe standing by the fore rail. I picked it up and busted off the winch handle with it. Then I handed the man two dollars and said he shouldn't even try to fix that winch handle as long as some fool was sitting over there shooting a rifle across the river. I led the Morgan around behind the shed to saddle him.

When I was remounted I dug heels in and lit out of there at a dead run. I heard Joshua fire again as I broke cover, but I had moved uphill a bit to come out at an unexpected spot and the shot came nowhere near. With the Morgan enjoying the run, I headed on up the hill, around the bend and down into the Plum Creek flats.

It was another two miles to where the road crossed the Plum at a shallow gravel bed. Stepped shale banks raised their thin shoulders barely above the icy water. I turned upstream, walked the horse along the creek bed for a few minutes, and then came out on a rocky bank and followed its course on upstream until about midmorning. It was spitting snow again and a wind had come up before I found another road and turned west, well into Illinois by this time.

Thomasboro was a cold bed in a barn loft while the tired Morgan munched sorghum grain in a snug stall below. In Hellett I shared a stall with the horse and on the outskirts of Bleekerville we both settled for a shed—but it had a good warm stove in it.

Then on a slate-grey noontime we came to Springfield, and a grander town I had never seen. Pa had spoken of the great cities of the East, and I had a notion this was what they must be like. There were more than a hundred buildings of one kind and another all snugged in together in the middle, while others straggled off north and south along the cleared tracks where steam locomotives could run.

There was a main street and several back streets, with crossways connecting them. And off beyond the far corner was a whole separate set of structures, big fine houses where important people must live. Even on that bleak day it was a glorious sight to see.

I was walking the Morgan along the main street, just looking around and seeing the sights, when a man on the walkway said, "Hey, Hooper, look at the farmer with the big gun!" I turned and he was looking right at me, pointing and laughing.

The one he had called to was just a few steps away, and he was laughing too. They were a sharp-looking pair with spat britches and bright ties, and I could see they were just spoiling for trouble. But I had all the trouble I needed right then, so I just looked them over and then ignored them. As I passed, the one called Hooper, a dandy with a dueling pistol sticking out of a red sash at his middle, made a crack about hill boys and shooting irons. If it had been some other time they would have had their fun. I would have seen to it. But not right now.

The town was packed with people, seemed like. Listening around, I picked up that there was politicking going on and a lot of folk had come in special to get in on the speechmaking and celebrations and fights. There was that Mr. Lincoln, the Whig ex-congressman, who was probably going to be president, the way the Democrats had bogged down. A lot of folks were in town for a look at him. And there were a lot of others, some tall at the trough and others not so, but all of them just politicking their heads off. There was a surprising lot of talk about the Kansas Free State votes.

I had read some in the newspapers, but in Indiana we didn't pay too much mind to the shenanigans of other people in other places. Here in Illinois, though, it seemed like people took politics personal.

It was a little hard to see how places like Kansas and such, way out there, could be such an issue here.

I found a livery stable with a stall to spare and space for a bedroll over by the stove, then went looking for a meal. About halfway down the street there was a saloon that served food. It didn't look like much but it smelled like they could cook. There was a long table in the back with stools along both sides, and I pulled one up and ordered a beefsteak when the kitchen swamper came around.

I was sitting with my back to the wall. There were a couple of workmen across and down from me, and at the end of the table a quiet, pleasant-looking fellow with an armband sat drinking coffee. My food had just been set before me when I saw those two hecklers from the street come in at the front door.

They were heading for the bar over at one side when the red-sashed one looked around and saw me and his face lit up. He nudged the other and said something and grinned, then they headed my way. It seemed like those old boys just couldn't leave well enough alone.

When they got to the table the first one walked right up and looked me over with his eyes kind of slanty and said, "Farm boy, I believe I'd like to look at that revolving pistol you've got."

I wanted to oblige him, up to a point. I stood up, turned a little so he could see the Walker clearly, then sat down again and went back to my dinner. He got red in the face.

"Maybe you didn't hear me, farmer. I said I want to look at that gun." He held out his hand. I ignored it and looked him right in the eye.

"Now why," I asked as pleasantly as anybody might, "would you be wanting to look at other people's weapons?"

The workmen across the table exchanged a glance, picked up their plates, and went to eat somewhere else. The rest of the room had quieted down a little. The one called Hooper moved up beside his friend and said, "He's a sassy one now, ain't he, Clay?" Then without a pause he pulled that dueling pistol out of his sash and pointed it at me.

"My friend wants to look at that there pistol, farmer, and he don't want any back talk. Now stand up, just easy, and do like I tell you."

There wasn't any other choice that I could see. I laid down my fork and stood up and before my knees came straight I had the muzzle of that Walker about two inches from his face, cocked and ready to fire. His eyes got about the size of walnuts and went crossed, from both of them trying to look down that big bore at the same time. Clay gasped.

"Mister," I told him, "back home I was taught it isn't polite to point, but you pointed first. Now this gun is ready to go off if I twitch my finger and it sure would splatter that wall over there if it did."

It was his move. He just stared into the Walker's muzzle and laid his dueling pistol down on the table.

"Put the other one there, too, why don't you," I said, keeping the tone of the conversation real friendly. He reached around behind his back, under his coat, and brought out another dueling pistol and laid it down. Anybody knows those things usually come in twos. Then I flicked the Walker around so the other fellow, Clay, could have a good look down inside it.

"I'm showing you my gun, sir, now I'd be obliged if you would show me yours."

He stuck a shaking hand inside his coat, pulled out a mean little pepperbox, and put it down on the table. Then I withdrew the Walker, let the hammer down, and turned it sideways, holding it up in front of them.

"This is a Walker Colt, gentlemen. Most of them went to the army back in '48 but this one was given to my pa. It shoots a .44 caliber ball on fifty grains of powder and it carries six loads." I shifted it around at them again and they both stiffened up. "Now if you gentlemen would be pleased to go about your business, my dinner is getting cold."

They went away, leaving their guns there on the table. When they were gone I put the Walker away and got back to my beefsteak. There hadn't been another sound in that room from the time I drew the gun, but the noise began again now, everybody trying to talk at once. Over across the way a little bug-eyed fellow was scribbling furiously on a paper tablet.

I was shoveling good food into my face when I heard a chuckle from the end of the table. The pleasant-looking man was still sitting there, his eyes sparkling now with mirth.

"That," he said, "was the damndest thing I ever saw."

I had to admit, I had sort of enjoyed it myself.

That was how I came to meet Hazen Burnett.

We got ourselves introduced and he moved around to where we could talk. When he stood I noticed he wore a Colt's revolver, but a smaller, newer one than my big old Walker. It was one of those slick Dragoon Colts, in a tooled holster just left of his belt buckle so the walnut-gripped brass butt stuck out from the open flap of his coat, very handy.

"You have shown me the error of my ways, Jeremy Burke," he said with a laugh in his voice. "I have maintained that the Whitneyville Walker revolver has no value as a belt arm, for being too big to draw quickly and too clumsy to use."

"Suits me all right," I said.

"Yes, I noticed. I wouldn't have missed that for the world." He reached into a waist pocket, brought out a set of tools, picked up one of the dueling pistols, and extracted the load. He put the gun back exactly where it had been and picked up another one.

"Are you in town for the politics, Mr. Burke, or just passing through?"

Passing through, I told him, and he shrugged. He was a husky, easy-looking man with a quiet humor about him. The manner of him and the set of his features were mild. But his eyes were about as mild as ice on the river, and just the same color.

I had the feeling there was more than just a casual question in his casual question. Pa always used to impress on us that it pays to be perceptive, and I learned early he was talking about more than how the road lays or where the stumps are in the field. He was talking about people. People always say more than they're saying if you learn to listen with your eyes while you're listening with your ears. Burnett had reason, I gathered, to want to know who I was and why I was there and how come I could use a pistol that way.

"More pilgrims than citizens in Springfield right

now," he commented. "I don't suppose you're here to meet a train?"

I wasn't certain whether he meant a regular train, like a wagon train, or one of those locomotive things, but either way I wasn't, and said so.

"There is an expedition making up for Kansas soon," he said. "Settlers coming through from the East." Those mild, cool eyes were feeling me out. "I don't suppose you're going to Kansas?"

I said I hadn't thought of it, and looked up, and decided I had had enough of that scrutiny. Just in those few minutes I came to understand something about Hazen Burnett. This was a man it would be better not to have reason to be afraid of. At the same time, I didn't feel any need to be explaining myself to a comparative stranger, so I thought I would just clear the air.

"Mr. Burnett, I gather that you gather that my being in Springfield at the same time you are in Springfield might mean I'm here for some reason related to whatever reason you are here. Is that right?"

Pa always used to say I had a two-dollar tongue, and swore I never got it from his side of the family. What he meant was that I could always twist words around to come up with two heads or two tails at the same time, or one of each if that was what was needed. That wasn't quite right, though. It was just that I had grown up knowing several things that kept me out of trouble. Like, if you are bigger than most of those around you, the odds are against you because the littler ones will always try you on for size, and if you lose, you lose because they won, and if you win, you lose because they're smaller. And like, words can be used to confuse as well as to clarify, and the best way to do either is to say exactly what you mean. And like, most uncomfortable situations can be avoided if one or the other party involved becomes confused enough to let the other party slip out of the situation without either party losing face.

Like that.

I had found a man can skin out of most potential troubles before they ever become troubles. Generally, whoever I double-tongued became just slightly confused. Burnett was no exception.

"How's that again?" he asked.

"I said," I said, "that I'm not in Springfield for any reason that you would be interested in either way, and I know that's what you want to know, so we can both relax."

He relaxed and the inquisitive element I had felt went out like a snuffed candle. He was satisfied, except that there was something in the twitch of his mouth—a quick, come-and-go sort of a grin—that said I had scored a point and he owed me one. At any rate, the edge was gone. He picked up his coffee and looked up at a man approaching the table. "Hello, Artemis, what's news today?"

It was the bug-eyed little fellow who had been writing in the tablet. He smiled a nervous, on-and-off smile and flicked a hand at the stool across from me. "May, uh, I join you, gentlemen?"

Burnett gestured broadly. "Do sit down, Artemis. Delighted to see you." Then he shot me a glance with a trace of deviltry in it. "Jeremy, may I introduce the excellent Artemis Steen, emissary from the fourth estate . . . Mr. Steen, be pleased to meet Jeremy Burke, newly arrived."

The little man was half seated. His hand shot out abruptly and I shook it for him. "Oh, I am indeed," he said, finally sitting down and hauling out his tablet and pencil from a bulging coat pocket.

He only hesitated a moment, then jumped right into what was on his mind. "I couldn't help observing the occurrence of a few minutes before," he explained. "Tell me, Mr. Burke, are you a paladin?"

He pronounced it *pah-la-deen* and I turned it around two or three other ways in my head but it still didn't mean anything.

"Oh, I can see you are, yes," he pressed on, then stopped and scribbled something on his pad of paper, and I finally got a handle on that word, paladin. That's like a knight errant, only Persian.

Steen finished writing, crossed a *T*, and looked up again. "If I may say so, Mr. Burke, your attire has the look of the hardy frontier about it. You come from the West, I imagine."

"I'm a farmer. From Indiana."

He looked pained for an instant, then brightened. "Ah, indeed, one of your adventurous persuasion would not wish to say overmuch about his travels. Yes, uh, obviously a frontiersman. Indians?"

"Eh?"

Burnett almost choked on his coffee.

"I say, uh, I venture you have been fighting the redmen, have you not? What tribe, if I may ask? Certainly not Sac and Fox, but possibly the Kaskaskia?" He thought it over, nodded, and began writing again. I had turned to Burnett for help, but he was giving his full attention to something across the room.

"Are you going to Kansas, Mr. Burke?" Steen paused only for a quick breath. "Indeed there should be opportunities there for a practitioner of the martial arts. Jayhawkers, border ruffians, the vote coming up and all . . . just imagine!" His enthusiasm threatened to overcome him. "Discovering an unheralded paladin, and in Springfield! Imagine!" He wrote something else.

"And bound for Bleeding Kansas. Wonderful! My editor will be pleased with this, indeed." He fixed me with the full sincerity of those bugged eyes. "He has encouraged me, you know, to go west and pursue my subject."

"Your subject?"

"Yes. *The New Paladins*. Do you realize, Mr. Burke, that you are the forerunner of an emerging breed?"

I hadn't realized anything of the kind.

"Mercenaries," he explained. "Mercenaries of a new variety. Knights errant of the revolving handgun. Paladins of the pistol . . . uh, yes, just a moment." With one finger in the air he paused to write something in his tablet, then nodded. "My subject is prodigies, you know. The men who are emerging in our troubled land possessed of a formidable skill with the handgun surpassing even, ah, the deadly arts of the fencing master.

"Do you know, Mr. Burke, that I have interviewed Elijah Walker himself on the subject? Yes, and Benjamin Furness and Boston Bill Hoot as well, not to mention Mr. Ernest Kichener, who is probably the epitome of the field. And now yourself, Mr. Burke. Tell me." He leaned closer. "How many men have you shot down?"

Up to that point he had been simply weird, but now he was meddling. I was not pleased with myself about poor Joey Sutton. I told him flatly it was none of his damned business, and instead of taking offense he was delighted.

"Excellent, sir, excellent. The answer of a true paladin. I may indeed have the material here soon for a truly definitive work on a new subject." He paused, studied his notes, then nodded in satisfaction. "Paladins of the pistol, yes. Very good. Duelists, of course, pistoleers, even 'shootists' might, ah . . ."

"Gunfighters?" Burnett suggested mildly.

The cranky-looking kitchen swamper was working our way with a great, blackened coffee pot and I waved him over to refill our cups. Steen mulled over Burnett's suggestion.

"Ah, possibly so," he admitted, "though I believe I prefer paladin, if I may. More romantic, you see, a certain exotic flair to it. The semanticist's burden, you know, ah, quite rigid, yes."

Abruptly Steen's head popped up and he turned, recognizing some voice across the room. He crammed the tablet back into his pocket, thumbed through some others there, and pulled one out. "If you will excuse me, gentlemen? And, uh, Mr. Burke, I would like to continue this interview at a later time if I may?"

When he was gone Burnett leaned back and grinned. I had tried confusion on him before, and then had run into a better confuser.

"You have just been interviewed," he said, "by one of Horace Greeley's best. Artemis Steen is like that all the time. He's a traveling correspondent for the *New York Tribune*.

"You may find yourself famous, Jeremy Burke, just because of him."

CHAPTER THREE

It soaked through later on that Artemis Steen had claimed I was a mercenary, and I didn't like that idea at all. For the rest of it I guessed Steen was harmless enough. Steen was what you might call an interpretative reporter, which is a whole different breed from regular newspaper reporters. A reporter writes things like they are. An interpretative reporter makes things up and then writes them the way he would have them be.

Most of that about "paladins" and "pistol prodigies" was just harmless fun with fancy words and no harm done. But the business about mercenaries wasn't funny. A mercenary is a kill-dog with no pack loyalty. He is a loner who goes where he can get the biggest bone. I never was one of those and I had a notion that, despite Kichener's and Hoot's reputations, they weren't, either. I thought it might be interesting to see their eyes. Pa used to say people's eyes tell their story if you know how to read them.

I had seen the eyes of killers twice before that I knew of. One was Martin Bethune, the Sand Creek killer, after they caught him down on the Siloh Flats. They brought him through Burnham on the way up to Hammond, and they stopped by our place for water.

The other was a gimp-leg little fellow by the name of Rinker, settled in near Veedersburg. He was a quiet man, kept to himself, but the word got around he had been to the war in the Crimea. And another story made the rounds, too. Rinker had killed fourteen men over there, and only done six of them with a gun.

Of the two, Rinker always struck me as the more dangerous, though I never knew him to do harm to anybody. It was in the eyes. That Martin Bethune, he was a berserker. His eyes were cloudy and full of hate, with little fires burning in them like a man insane. But Rinker's eyes didn't have anything in them at all. They were empty and cold. Talking to him you knew there was somebody in there, and his manner was mild and unassuming. But you couldn't see him through those eyes.

Burnett told me before we parted that I could pick up wages if I wanted to stay around Springfield for a few days. The town marshal was looking for another man to help out while all the crowds were in town. Burnett was patrolling for him, but he needed another and wasn't having much luck finding one. It was interesting. I had a little money, but not enough for comfort. But the thought of Joshua Sutton came to me and I decided I would move on tomorrow. It would be like that crazy Joshua to drop everything and follow me clear across Illinois just to get a shot at me.

A long train of brand-new overland wagons had come through town while I was having dinner, and I could see them now out beyond the edge of town, formed up in neat rows on a little patch of high ground. Men were scurrying around out there unhitching stock and moving them across to where there was a string fence around a field of good winter graze and a little thaw-water pond. Those big wagons looked pretty out there in their military ranks. They had the look of far places about them.

A lot of the people hurrying along the streets, the ones newly arrived from back east, would be aboard those wagons soon, packed and rolling high, heading for their promised land. I was thinking that I might see some of the same faces again sometime at the far end of the western road if I went that way. I was so intent on the sight of those wagons that I walked square into someone and knocked her down on the boardwalk.

She was a slight-built, blond-haired girl in a green satin dress, and when I bumped her she sat right down with a thump and the packages she was carrying went every which way.

When her eyes got refocused she gasped and said, "Oh!" in a soft voice, and I pulled off my hat and knelt down by her. Other people around had stopped to look, but started moving on again, going about their business. I gathered in some of the packages and was reaching for one off to the side when a small hand darted from behind somebody's legs and grabbed it. A shirttail boy with torn britches clutched the parcel to his breast and ran. I shouted after him but he was already gone.

I asked the girl if she was all right and offered a hand but she ignored it and picked herself up. I said again, "I'm sorry, ma'am."

"It's miss," she said, cool and irritated. "And yes, I am all right, no thanks to you."

I stooped to pick up the packages piled at her feet and my shoulder bumped her as I leaned, and she backed up a couple of steps, getting her balance.

"Great heavens! You're dangerous."

I handed the packages over to her. They were soiled and rumpled from the fall. "Yes, ma'am . . . miss, I guess I am at that."

Several men were hanging around, probably to make sure I didn't offend the lady any more than I already had. I said again how sorry I was and she looked over her pitiful parcels, got another pained expression, and said, "Don't think of it," then whipped on down the street, head high.

I was still standing there holding my hat when I remembered the other package. I had to run to catch her, and when she heard me coming she turned, gasped, and backed off, holding the parcels in front of her for protection. But I stopped several feet away.

"Don't worry, miss. I won't hit you anymore. I wanted to tell you, a boy ran off with one of your sacks back there."

She looked to her burdens and her brows went up. "Oh, dear. My linen."

"Never you mind, miss, I'll find it for you or get you some more. Who should I deliver it to?" She started to protest or huff, one or the other, but I added, "Please?"

"My name is Puckett, sir. Eleanor Puckett. We are staying at the Walsh house." Then she hurried away.

There was no chance of finding the tad who ran off with that bundle, so I began going to stores. At the third place they remembered Miss Puckett and her purchases.

When the man found out I wanted to replace the linens the girl had lost, but I didn't know how much of it there was, he put a hand to his chin and made an issue out of remembering. Then he sold me about twice as much as she probably had in the first place. I didn't argue. It was amends for knocking her on her dignity like that.

I located the Walsh house. When I got there a

large woman with red hair answered the door, disapproved of my attire, took the package, and said she would see that Miss Puckett got it. I asked if Miss Puckett was kin of hers.

"She and her father are staying here as guests," she said, indicating a "Rooms For Let" sign at the porch rail. I had come up the side path and hadn't noticed it.

"Are they staying long?"

She looked suspicious, but apparently I didn't sound as rough as I looked to her. "Only until the wagon train makes up," she said finally.

I had started down the steps when an impulse caught me. I turned. "Mrs. Walsh?"

She peered through the nearly closed door.

"Do you have a vacant room?"

"Ask me when you are presentable," she said and closed the door.

All the way back to the main part of town I had the picture in mind of a pretty face with blond hair around it and big, startled blue eyes. It took me a while to find Burnett. He was up the street a ways, watching some carpenters putting up a big platform out in the middle of an intersection. I told him I had changed my mind about the constable job and he said, in that dry way of his, "I gather you ran into someone persuasive."

Burnett walked me over to the marshal's office. That gentleman wasn't very impressed, but when Hazen Burnett vouched for me, I got signed on for a day-to-day basis. "Parade duty," the marshal called it.

His first order was that I should get into some clothes that wouldn't disgrace his town. Then he handed me a sheaf of yellow papers and asked if I could read. I expect I could have read circles around him, but I decided that would be a premature judgment and just said yes.

"Then you take these and read them," he said. "These are the ordinances of the city of Springfield. You pick out the main ones and memorize them and if you see anybody doing them you make them stop. Is that clear?"

"Yes, sir."

"All right. Be here first thing in the morning to go to work. And get rid of those." He pointed at the clothes I was wearing. "You look like a Hoosier."

Outside I asked Burnett what a Hoosier was but I guess he didn't know either.

That evening, after a bath and a shave, and wearing new clothes that were stiff and scratchy and new boots that still had the proud in them, I went back to Mrs. Walsh's house. I had already signed and paid for a room before she figured out that she had seen me before. Then she put her hands on her hips and said, "Well! I wouldn't have believed it."

"Supper's at six o'clock," she said, "so you've already missed it. You can get a bite uptown if you want. Places there that don't ever close, though they ought to be shut down for good, most of them.

"Breakfast is at five in the morning, and you'll use the back door when you go in and out. No single men allowed in the parlor. The ladies have tea there and I'll not have giggling and goggling in my house. Is that clear?"

"Yes, ma'am."

"Very well. Your room is second on the left, upstairs."

"Yes, ma'am. And which is Miss Puckett's room?"

She frowned at that and said, "Nowhere near

yours, you may be sure, Mr. Burke. Good night to you now, and don't make any noise when you come in. I have guests who enjoy their sleep."

I found a saloon downtown that was wide open and roaring with business, and managed to crowd in and find a table. All they could feed was fried beef and cornbread, but I was hungry enough that it could have been prime smoked ham for all the difference it would have made.

When I was full I sat back with a big mug of lukewarm black coffee to watch the raucous doings in the place. A lot of men were in there, making a lot of noise and drinking a lot of spirits.

I never had much opportunity before to witness the drinking of spirits as a social phenomenon, but Pa always allowed it was interesting to watch. You learn a lot about folks that way, he said. Pa maintained that the effect of spirits was to dull the thinking processes layer by layer. That which was shallowest went first and that which was deepest stayed longest. The result, he felt, was that spirits revealed what the real person underneath was like.

No matter what veneer he wears, a feisty person, when he's had a couple, will act feisty, a mean person will act mean, a generous person will act generous, and like that. That is the social level in imbibery, Pa always said. Beyond that is another level, which is pure drunk.

The social level of imbibery was in full swing in that saloon and there were raw personalities poking through all over the place. There were jokes being told, arguments being had, bets being made, and tall tales being stretched all at once.

It sounded as though the place might explode into a riot at any moment, but there wasn't much hostility about most of it, just a bunch of men letting off steam and relaxing in a warm place on a cold night.

There was one situation, though, over by the bar, that looked touchy.

A teamster was leaning on the counter top there, drinking alone, and next to him a cross-grained fellow was also drinking alone. Both of them looked like they had been at it for a while, and that cross-hatched one was spoiling for trouble just as surely as anybody I ever saw.

You can usually tell, if you know the signs, when a man is about ready to blow up, and this one was at that point. Once, for instance, somebody coming through passed close to him and jostled him a bit. Normally, in a crowded place, if a fellow gets bumped he just moves over a little to accommodate. But not this one. Quick as that he swung around and had a fist cocked back to let fly, but the man who brushed him had moved on, never noticing, and there was nobody there to hit.

He turned back to his drink, but there was no doubt about it. That one was stretched about as thin as he could go. And he kept glancing at that teamster next to him, who just went on with his drinking, paying no mind.

There was some heavy gambling going on at one of the tables and I had turned to watch that when the trouble started. What happened was the teamster turned to lean one elbow on the bar and as he did he noticed a bug crawling on the floor by his boot. So he stepped on it. And the cross-grained one saw him do it.

He backed off a step, squared himself and said, "You low-life scoundrel!"

It was a minute before the teamster realized he was being talked to, but when it soaked in his brow went down and his shoulders went up. "Who you talking to, mister?"

"I'm talking to you, you slobbering oaf. You stepped on my bug."

Now that caught the teamster off guard. "I did what?"

"That bug!" The cross one pointed an accusing finger at the squashed remains. "That was my bug, and you stepped on it!"

There can be all kinds of fussing and bickering going on in a place like that and nobody pays much attention. But when the possibility of a real fight comes up, everything else just grinds to a halt. Just like that, everybody in the place knew something was going on at the bar and all those other conversations stopped. A little open space cleared around the two and somebody over by the wall commenced to offer odds on the teamster. That looked like a likely proposition. Though they were both big men with plenty of beef on them, and both about equally drunk, the teamster was just starting to get his blood up and the other one, whatever he was mad about, had been mad for quite a while. That gave the teamster an edge, it seemed to me.

I hadn't seen him come in, but suddenly Hazen Burnett was there by the door, close to them, and he got their attention. He had a pistol in his hand and he said, never raising his voice, "Gentlemen, before either of you says another word get rid of your weapons."

They both looked him over, and both obeyed.

"That's fine," Hazen said. "Now set them aside, and you may proceed with your discussion."

The teamster did as he was told. He laid his sheathed bowie knife on the bar and slid it away. The cross-grained one had pulled a horse pistol out of his coat and now, with an oath, he flung it sidehand across the room. I had call to notice that pistol because it thudded onto the table where I sat, skidded across and knocked half a mug of black coffee over into my lap. And my lap had brand-new britches on it.

Hazen had backed off, satisfied, and the two were squaring off again, and there I was wet from the waist down, coffee stained, and getting madder by the second. A fellow ought to stay out of things that are none of his business, but those were brand-new clothes.

As I stood up the cross one was saying, "I said that was my bug, and you had no right to kill it."

"Hell, I'll get you another bug," the teamster bellowed, "but you got some apologizing to do first, mister."

I was more interested in my clothes than in their fight, so I handed my gunbelt to Hazen and waded right in. The cross one wanted trouble and I was ready to accommodate him to the tune of a new pair of trousers. The first problem was to separate those two and do it in such a way that cross-grain would still be fit to negotiate with.

He had just drawn back for a roundhouse swing at the teamster when I got to him. I grabbed him by the back of his coat and heaved backward. He followed through with his swing, but it was about a foot short of connecting with anybody. And before he could collect his balance I hollered right in his ear, "Hold on, there, man, that fellow just saved your life!"

He was a little slow on the uptake. "Who did? Him?"

"That's right, he just saved your life, if you didn't know it."

Both of them were staring at me kind of stupid now, and everybody else in the place was looking puzzled.

"Didn't you take a close look at your bug before you brought him in here?" I made it sound real accusing, and pointed at the splatter of bug on the board floor. He looked, along with everybody else, then shook his head.

"Well, sir, it's time you did. See that foam there? Mister, that bug was rabid!"

Now he was starting to catch up with me and he said, "Awww," and squinted around, but I kept his attention.

"Just look at it. Any fool can see that's a hydrophoby bug. And it was crawlin' right for you when your friend here tromped it. Mister, it's true. He saved your life."

He was peering closely at the bug now, skepticism working all over his face. "There ain't no such thing as a hydrophoby bug," he argued.

"Is that what you think? Then you must never have seen one before. Have you?"

"No."

"There, it's like I said. You just didn't know about them."

If he had been perplexed before, he was confused now. His fogged mind wasn't keeping up with it.

"I'll put it to Mr. Burnett, there," I told him. "Mr. Burnett, you've seen rabid bugs before, haven't you?"

Hazen didn't bat an eye. "Several," he said. "And that's one of the fiercest-looking ones I ever saw."

The cross fellow still looked like he suspected he was being had, but he wasn't sure. He was eyeing that flat bug like it was the first one he had ever seen.

"Now what we need to do," I told him seriously, "is find the other one. Where do you keep it?"

"The other what?"

"The other hydrophoby bug, man! That kind always goes in pairs, and if one's rabid they both are. Now out with it, before somebody gets bit. Where's your other bug?"

"I don't have any damn bug." His eyes were getting bigger and rounder by the minute. "That wasn't my bug, honest. I just said it was."

"Well now, that's bad," I told him. "If they aren't yours, that means they're rogue bugs. Wild ones. And those are the worst of all. I tell you," I confided in him, lowering my voice with urgency, "it looked like that one was makin' for your britches' leg. I'd wager the other one's already in there somewhere, hiding in a seam."

Suddenly he turned pale and began to tremble. "In my britches?"

I nodded. Before I could suggest he get out of them he was down to his long johns. He backed off quickly, leaving his britches there in a pile on the floor. "Somebody take a look, please," he said. But I shook my head. "Be better if nobody got too close," I told him. "You just had a real close call, and I wouldn't want to go fingerin' around in that cloth, myself."

There was a breathless silence in the room. The crowd was fascinated, waiting for whatever came next.

"There's only one thing to do," I told cross-grain flatly. "You got to burn them. Here's a match. Do it quick."

He didn't hesitate at all. He lit the match, tossed it, and in a minute those old britches were blazing up there on the floor.

"Man alive," I breathed. "That was a close one. But you surely got him."

He was staring dazedly at the fire. "That was my britches," he said.

I thought about it a minute. "Tell you what," I said. "If you've got the price of another pair on you, I'll run out and get you some. Hazen, is there a store open?"

"Scribner's place. Three doors down."

The fellow dug around in his coat pocket and came out with some coin. I took it, went down the street and got myself a new pair of britches. After I had changed I rolled up the old ones and went back to the saloon. Nobody had moved much to speak of. There was a hum of speculation, which died down when I came in the door.

I tossed my old pants to the ex-troublemaker, retrieved my gunbelt from Hazen, and strapped in on.

"They didn't come in your size, feller," I told the man, "so I got me some. You can have my old ones there. They ought to go most of the way around you and a piece of rope will do the rest. And don't worry about those stains all over them. That's coffee. You put it there and you can clean it out."

I was already out the door when somebody in there whooped, and then somebody else, and then it sounded like the whole place had exploded with laughter.

Hazen Burnett came up with me a ways down the street, and he was wiping tears out of his eyes. "Hydrophoby bug!" He almost choked. "That's the most outrageous thing I ever heard. Be interesting having you around, Jeremy Burke."

CHAPTER FOUR

Parade duty, as the constable called it, was just that: parading around town, patrolling the streets, watching the crowds, and watching for trouble.

It was one-time work but it paid well. Mostly, Springfield was a well-ordered place where a deputized constable and occasional notice from the sheriff kept things peaceful. Right then, though, it was a handful of a town.

A lot of those escaped New Englanders were in Springfield getting ready to form up their train for the trek to their new homes on Kansas soil. Also there were three kinds of politicians on hand: a few real true-life politicians who had either won office or were about to; then a larger bunch of grit-teeth-grinning second-runners watching the prime types to see how it was done; and then a still larger batch of hangers-on who made up a sort of retinue around each of the run-for-office ones. And there were hundreds of interested souls in from all over the countryside to hear the speeches, watch the fights, do a bit of shopping, and trade gossip. These last were the bulk of the crowd. They were ordinary folks, mostly, who'd show up for a political occasion or a gypsy circus, whichever came first, and in about the same spirit.

It was a new thing for me, watching that many people that riled up about things they couldn't do anything about except maybe vote. Now I know, as

Pa always told me, that a man's vote is his ticket to freedom, but I also know several folks back home, like Clyde Barley, who always make it a practice to vote two or three times on every issue and still don't really care how the count comes out. Politics in Indiana is a whole lot different thing than politics in Illinois. In Illinois they always capitalize the *P*, or maybe capitalize on it, whichever. Back there along Sugar Creek we'd never considered politics much to talk about.

But there certainly was talk in Springfield. There was dark muttering about how much the precinct judges made off their fines and how it was time to spread the wealth. There was candid evaluation of the nincompoopery of the state legislature. And there was gloomy speculation about the foibles of those tarnished saviors on the Potomac, which ones were going bad and which were outright rotten and how you should draw the line.

And there was a particular subject woven throughout the fabric: the issue of slavery. The cotton empires in the South had just about outgrown this institution, as their northern neighbors had a generation earlier, until along came somebody and paid Mrs. Stowe to write a book on the subject and all of a sudden it was the hottest issue of the day, hot enough, apparently, to draw attention away from what the northeast interests were trying to do to the southern interests in Washington.

A lot of people felt the issue was being resolved to the west, in Kansas.

Hazen Burnett was doing the same thing I was doing, parade duty. He worked one part of town while I worked another.

When our paths crossed we would howdy and change notes and then go on our ways. Burnett wasn't a Springfield native any more than I was. He was from Freeport, down the road a good bit, but he knew quite a few of the regular folks in Springfield and could fill me in on them. Right now, he was planning on joining that train for Kansas. He would draw wages from the colony to look after them along the way. There had been real trouble out that way, and he said they were paying for combination guards and guides. He had an itch to go west and break some fresh ground, and it was a good deal for him.

I was curious why those settlers were making up in Springfield and going west overland instead of the usual route of taking the rivers to Westport and jumping off from there. He didn't know exactly, except this was the way the organizers of the colony had decided it was to be. They were going to have to ferry two big rivers to get to Kansas, but that was how they wanted to do it.

"Look at them down there by their wagons," he said pointing. Off beyond the edge of town forty or fifty men were working over the big wagons while others tended the draft stock. "They look like farmers, don't they?"

They did, and I allowed that's what they were.

"Well, I guess most of them think that, too," he said. "But as far as Mark Hayden and his land company are concerned, those folks are seed to be planted to sow a crop of money."

We met one time at the door of a hashery, drank some hot coffee and went our ways from there, and I hadn't gone a block when I saw the constable hurrying toward me.

"You watch close today, Burke," he snapped. "We got bushwhackers in town."

"Here?" I asked because it didn't seem likely.

There were bushwhackers over west in Missouri and on the Kansas border, but right in the middle of peaceable Illinois?

"You damn right, here!" He was nervous. "There's a bunch of them from over on the *Sentinel* in town right now, sizin' up these Jayhawkers. You watch close now, you hear?"

He headed off to find Hazen Burnett and I went on down the street, very much aware of the yellow arm band I was wearing. It struck me how heavy a little piece of cloth—or a badge for that matter—can get to be. Bushwhackers—wild outlaws from the Missouri hills—were a strong draught of responsibility for a day-to-day deputy constable. Back along Sugar Creek, now, I had got to know some pretty wild folk: not the ones that had socials and howdied in town, but the ones that came roaring in once in a blue moon from Turkey Run and down there, that would as soon slit your gizzard as eat persimmon pie. I even stomped one of them a little bit one time just to let him know he wasn't to come near our place. But those hellers back there just seemed like crossways home folks compared to the stories I'd heard about the Missouri raiders.

About then a vision appeared down the street fit to put such musings out of my head. She was wearing bright blue gingham, a heavy grey shawl, and a red scarf with a stray blond curl peeking out of it. She was helping her father herd an obtuse old brindle cow toward the stock lot at the edge of town and they were having problems. In true cow fashion, that brindle wanted to go everywhere except where it was supposed to. And it was a determined enough cow that a crippled old man and a skirt-tangled girl were no match for it.

It could have been an act of kindness to give them

a hand. Actually it was nothing of the sort. I had my eye on the pretty face and gentle attentions of Miss Eleanor Puckett, and I hadn't done well at all in my campaign. Getting a room at the boarding house where she was staying had seemed a good idea, but in two days I had hardly seen her there. And between the gimlet eye of Mrs. Walsh and the sour face of old man Puckett I was becoming distinctly uncomfortable around there. I had the feeling of a fox paying room rent in a chicken house and then finding all the chickens are locked up someplace else.

So giving them a hand now with the brindle cow was in the finest tradition of chivalry. I was seeking the attention of the fair maiden, and her crippled old father could go hang.

I tipped my hat, offered my services, and took a switch to that cow. She didn't like it a bit but she went, and when I had her safely gated into the pasture I tipped my hat again, gave Miss Puckett my best smile, and headed back into town. Behind me I heard her say, "Thank you, sir," and then a scolding "Pa!" And a moment later the old man's reluctant voice said, "Mister."

I turned and he glared at me. "Obliged," he said, finally.

The sun broke through the clouds about midafternoon that day, right on schedule, and pretty soon there were crowds on the street and bright bunting flapping on the big speaking platform out front of the hotel. It was the first real sunshine in a week or more and it busted through those miserable clouds and sent them scudding from the sky. Bright hues laced through the sharp air with a promise of distant spring.

Before long the politicians descended upon the middle of town and the speeches began. There were several of them with a claim to the podium, and I drifted along to where the main crowd was, watching people and listening to oratory. All of it on this day had to do with the main issue of the Kansas-Nebraska Act, the institution of slavery. Now me, I'd never been a slave nor owned one either, and I guessed most of those around me didn't know any more about it than I did. But there was a fervor about it, and real politicking is never hindered by a lack of knowledge.

The main talker of the day, waiting his turn, was a gaunt beanpole of a man who stood ears and eyebrows above most of the crowd even before he mounted the platform. He was Abraham Lincoln, and he had been in the Congress once, and he was pushing to go back to Washington with slavery as his issue. I noted a thing about him that appealed to me. Standing still he appeared awkward and clumsy. But he moved with the grace of a woodsman and there was power in those long, bony limbs.

When he climbed up on the platform he towered above the crowd, and when he opened his mouth the voice that came out was high-pitched and rasping—a squeaky kind of voice that you wouldn't have expected from a man that size. But it carried. The words rang along that crowded street as though they came clear up from his big boots.

He started slowly, talking about the sanctity of people's right to make their own choices. Then his volume built up as he said, "But when that process produces interference with the exercise of that same right by others, then the public conscience must in justice supercede!"

He went on, making some sense along the way, and I was letting it soak in when I turned to check the crowd and saw a face that froze me where I stood.

Across the way, beyond the crowd, Joshua Sutton was coming out of the post office. As I watched he glanced around at the people near him, then leaned against a porch post, relaxed and easy. He hadn't spotted me.

I had come this far to avoid a run-in with the Suttons, and I didn't want one now. I eased back into the crowd, hunched down a little, and worked my way right up close to the speaker's platform. I wanted to slide around behind and get out of sight, but I was boxed in by the crowd there and didn't want to raise a commotion. I couldn't see Joshua through the crowd, but then he couldn't see me either. What I had in mind was to ease around to where I could come up behind him, then take that rifle away from him, rattle his teeth a bit, and send him on back home where he belonged. But I didn't get that done. Right at the wrong time that crowd of folks shifted to let a man lead his mule through, and when I looked there was wide open space between me and Joshua.

I saw him and he saw me. For just an instant his jaw sagged, then he grinned and swung that old long rifle to his shoulder. Joshua Sutton never did have any sense. He thumbed the hammer back as the gun came level, and I had nowhere to go. Even then I suppose I could have nailed him where he stood, but all I could think of was Pa's feeble words back there on that cold hillside: "Don't ever shoot a Sutton, boy. Promise me."

I promise, Pa. I do.

Joshua had his rifle up and sighted and there were startled exclamations as some of those around him saw what was happening. Then somebody slammed into my shoulder, jarring my teeth, and both of us stumbled to the side. It was Hazen Burnett.

While the crash of Joshua's rifle was still echoing, splinters showering from the wood railing where I had been, Burnett had turned cat-quick and had his Colt in his hands, fire belching from it. I saw Joshua dive for cover, losing himself in the scurrying remnants of the crowd on that side.

What happened next made no sense at all. As I got my feet under me there was a flash from an upstairs window, another rifle cracked, and a ball whipped past my ear. By pure reflex I shucked the Walker and when it spoke the man who fell back from that window with a .44 ball through his head was no one I knew. He was a stranger.

Two more men had run out of a door across the street. One had a rifle to his shoulder, aiming at the platform over my head. A gun barked somewhere and the man went down. The other one turned and started to run, then turned back and raised his rifle just as Hazen Burnett came up beside him. Hazen brought his pistol down across the fellow's forearm and I could hear the bones snap clear across the street. The man hollered, dropped his rifle, and went stumbling off around the corner of the building. Another shot was fired up the street somewhere, beyond the scurrying crowd, and I heard a scattergun roar. Then there were hoofbeats, several horses, going away in a hurry.

It was all over in seconds. By the time most of the crowd got started scattering, by the time the politicians on the platform got started down the steps, the shooting was all done. I noticed, the way you'll notice odd things in an instant of pressure, that Mr. Lincoln didn't hurry. He even stepped back to let someone else get to the stairs ahead of him.

There had been six shots fired in all. A man lay dead on the snowy walk in front of Gordon's Haberdashery, and over beyond the platform, in the street, a pudgy man in a frock coat was down on his knees, blood spreading across the back of his coat.

I stood in the street, gun up, trying to see everything at once. Hazen Burnett had disappeared around the haberdashery, after the man with the broken arm. A little way off the constable stood spread-legged in the middle of an intersection, turning slowly, surveying his town. He had a big, double-barreled shotgun at the ready.

All along the way doors were slamming as the last of the spectators disappeared. Some horses at a hitchrail were skittering around, ears up and the whites of their eyes showing, and just beyond them an empty springboard wagon was heeled over against a curb, its horse fouled in the traces.

For a moment then the street was nearly deserted and the only sound was the moaning of the backshot man by the platform. Then a few folks started sticking their heads out of doors, and a few hardy ones came back out to see what was going on. I walked across to look at the dead man on the walk. He had been a medium-sized man of about thirty-five, but he wasn't anything now. Someone had put a hole squarely through his heart. I had never seen him before.

A young fellow with a visor on his head peered out of the post office, then came out cautiously, seeing my yellow arm band.

"I saw it start," he said. "The man who shot first was in the post office just a few minutes ago, asking after someone. He stepped outside. I came to the window to watch the speaking, and that fellow raised his rifle and shot right at the platform."

My throat felt dry. "Was he asking about me, by any chance?"

"Are you Mr. Burke? If you are, then he was."

Someone nearby said, "He was after you, then?"

"Yes. His name is Joshua Sutton. He's from back home and he's plain crazy. But I don't know any of the others. I never saw them."

The clerk's eyes were puzzled. "You just stood there when he cut down on you. You didn't even try to draw your gun?"

"Yes." I didn't want to talk about it right then. I pointed out the upstairs window where the sniper had been, and a couple of townsmen headed around the building toward a side stairway. A few seconds later one of them appeared in the open window and called, "This one's dead up here." I already knew that.

The constable was bending over the injured man in the street, and several men came forward to pick him up and carry him into a saloon. The constable came over to me. "What was it all about? Could you tell?"

I shook my head. "I know the one who shot first, is all. He was trying to shoot me, and he got away in the crowd. But I don't know the others. I don't think they were with him."

There was a commotion then, and Hazen Burnett came out of the alley dragging—half carrying—the man whose arm he had busted. Some citizens were tailing along after them, wide-eyed and curious. The constable looked him over, then sent them along to the saloon where the back-shot fellow had been taken.

"Doctor'll be there in a minute," he said. "Let's get these folks patched up, then find out what this was all about."

I noticed Artemis Steen scurrying around, asking questions, trying to see everything at once, filling page after page of a paper tablet.

CHAPTER FIVE

It took the better part of three days to get it cleared up to Springfield's satisfaction. And during those days some of us searched the town and the surrounding country for Joshua Sutton, but there was no sign of him.

The constable sent for the sheriff, a round and righteous man named Myers, and he got a judge to impanel a board of inquiry. Then most of us who had been there when the shooting happened were handed subpoenas.

Nobody was allowed into the hearing room except to testify, but the rest of Springfield and visiting humanity managed to put it together from gossip, piece by piece.

I might mention that the saddest part of it all to me was that whatever little favor I had previously won in the bright eyes of Eleanor Puckett was lost to me and I was back to taw. The story of the bug discussion in the saloon had made the rounds, and Mrs. Walsh had heard it and recounted it in no glamorous terms to her lady guests. Then there was the gunfight, and the next time I saw Eleanor her bright eyes held only a hard glare directed at me. I was a liar, a hoaxter, a flim-flam artist, and a gunman, and she added it all up and got nothing.

The first time I tried a conversation after that I was very finely snubbed. Mrs. Walsh looked victorious and Mr. Puckett looked relieved.

As to the shooting, most everybody in town knew exactly what had happened. The trouble was the things they knew were all different.

Most of the politicians and the lawyers were certain the whole thing had been set up as an assassination of one of them but they couldn't agree which one. The constable was pretty sure the town had been invaded by anti-abolitionist bushwhackers from Missouri.

The sheriff, who was a man noted for never taking a drink, was of the opinion that everybody involved had been drunk and the saloons should all be closed up.

When he included Burnett and me in that supposition the constable offered to hit him in the mouth for it. That constable was a man to stand up for his employes.

As it finally was resolved, most everyone was partly right except the politicians and the lawyers.

When the bailiff got around to calling me and I went into talk to the hearing jury, I judged by their questions they had things mostly sorted out, except for how the shooting started in the first place. I told them about Joshua Sutton looking for me, and why, and how Hazen had saved my life by pushing me aside when Joshua fired.

I related the rest of it as I had seen it, the man in the window, the ones on the street and all, and when they ran out of questions I was dismissed, and they called Hazen Burnett in next.

One of the extra lawyers in town was making himself some change by defending Abel Klotz, the man Burnett had busted there on the street, and the lawyer wouldn't let him go before the hearing board, because there were charges against him and that might bias his case. But Klotz had already said a good deal to the constable and some others before the lawyer got hold of him, and his comments explained a lot of it.

At any rate, the hearing panel finally wrote up a report to the judge and then got itself dissolved so its members could go back to work. The judge had the report copied and distributed to the sheriff and the constable so they could file their charges. And Mrs. Walsh invited the sheriff, the constable, the judge, and some of the panel members to her house for supper that night so she could be the first hostess to get the whole story.

The constable didn't talk much, nor did the judge, but that sheriff just opened up there at Mrs. Walsh's long table and told the whole thing, and that's how we heard the sum of it.

The strangers were, as it turned out, a bunch of renegade riders from over in Missouri who knew of the Jayhawker train making up in Springfield and had come all this way just to make some trouble. They probably had been planning to haze some farmers or run off some stock, or maybe burn a few wagons.

They had hung around town waiting for a good time, and had got nervous when some folks who knew them showed up. So they had held clear of the Jayhawker bunch, and had done some hard drinking to pass the time. The fact they were in town, liquored up and spoiling for trouble, just when Joshua Sutton started shooting, was pure coincidence. But when the shooting started they joined it. The man in the upstairs window probably thought it was one of his cronies being shot at down on the street.

There had been eight of them altogether, apparently. Two were dead, one was in jail with a broken arm, and the rest had high-tailed out of town when the party started. One of them had shot wild into the crowd and wounded an innocent bystander, and the constable had dusted them with birdshot on their way down the street.

They likely wouldn't be back.

Joshua Sutton had just disappeared, and I was not especially sorry. Of all the Suttons, he was always the downright mean one.

Like when all of us were just boys, if a couple of fellows got into a fracas and were going at it fists, teeth, and thumbnails out behind the schoolhouse, Joshua's sport was to wait until both of them were down and then rush up and start kicking kidneys and crotches, just for the hell of it. He never was particular who he kicked, but he always preferred the one on the bottom.

Some folks always thought maybe it was Joshua that blinded the Dunlap boy several years back, too. They'd had some hard words one day, and then later on the kid was out in his father's pasture after dark and somebody came slipping around a thicket and threw lye in his face. There was some talk about it, but nobody could exactly prove it was Joshua that had done it.

It was his style, though, and he didn't change any as he grew up.

There was a time I remember well, just a couple of years earlier, when Joshua had been hunting down in the bottoms, off in that solemn canyon country known as The Shades, and found a runaway Negro slave holed up down there in a cave.

The Negro was a big, strapping buck, black as spades and straight out of the Cuban docks, and come to find out later he was sold to a Tennessee flatlands planter and had run off the very day the man got him home. But at the time Joshua found him, he was half-starved and half-crazy with the cold and just hiding out there, big-eyed, in that hole.

Well, Joshua had heard the stories about slave hunters that got as much as a thousand dollars reward for every slave they brought in. So he'd taken that Negro out and tied him to a tree there in The Shades and then he mounted up and went to find him a slave hunter.

As it turned out, he did find one, over at Rockville. But it took him about three days to get there and back with the man. Meantime Aaron Sutton and I and a couple more met up with them on the Rockville road and followed along to see what was happening.

The Negro was still there when we got to The Shades. Joshua had tied him tight to that tree. I hope never to see again what tight ropes will do to a body in three days' time.

That slave hunter took one look, drew a gun, and shot the poor wretch dead. It was a mercy. And then to top it off, Joshua raised hell because the man had thrown away a reward that he considered half his by rights. I'll never forget that slave hunter's face. He was as tough a customer as you might hope to find, and he was rock-hard right to the core. But right then I halfway expected him to beat hell out of Joshua on general principles. And if he had, it would have been more for what Joshua had done to that pitiful Negro than for having wasted his time.

Anyway, that's how Joshua Sutton was, and I never cared for him at all.

The problem now was he knew where I was and I didn't know where he had gotten to.

The rest of my main problem was Joshua's brothers. I didn't figure Aaron to be coming after me on account of Joey's death back there in Indiana. He knew why that happened, and he wouldn't hold to it as an excuse the way Joshua had. But I remembered Aaron's words there in the cemetery, and I knew that if anything happened to Joshua I might have him to reckon with.

And then there was Sonny Sutton. You just never knew about Sonny, one way or another. I couldn't recall ever hearing him say more than three or four words all in one string, but when the action came he was always there. And like me, he favored a handgun.

I could feel my time in Springfield running out. I had made a practice of stopping by the livery a couple of times each day to look in on the Morgan, partly just to rub his muzzle and talk to him and assure him I was still around, partly to remind the livery keeper that it was worth his hide to mistreat the animal in any smallest manner.

Since the shooting, though, my visits to the stable were more with an eye to how ready the horse was for travel. And that good horse, as always, was ready and raring.

On a bright morning, with a touch of false spring in the air, I saddled him up and went for a ride.

Winter was clinging with icy determination to the shadow slopes of the breaks, and retreating slowly from the prairie lands as little rivulets of thaw formed here and there to soften the black earth in the hollows.

And that bright sun was climbing a little higher each day, promising that spring would come one day, and you could count on it.

From atop a long hogback swale a couple miles east of Springfield I watched the glittering, fuming progress of a steam locomotive coming in from the north, running down the valley slick as horses but a lot messier.

A mile or so out a bunch of local boys rode out on cantering spring-touched horses to meet the thing and race it back to town. From where I sat I could see a white puff of steam erupt from the boiler of the engine as those boys came up to it, wheeled their mounts, and went racing back toward town, cavorting along on the machine's flanks and cutting back and forth across the tracks ahead of it. A long time later I heard the distant whistle that those puffs of steam had cut loose.

There were three freight cars and two passenger coaches behind that shining engine. It was no match for the galloping horses in speed, but it was pulling a load all of them together couldn't have managed.

I sat there and watched them all the way into town, then heeled the Morgan and headed back in.

Among other folks, the wagon train committee had arrived, and there apparently was going to be no delay in setting out for Kansas. Long before I rode into town I could see the flurry of activity out in the west pasture, where people who had been waiting were now doing the last minute things to wagons and stock that signaled the beginning of travel.

At the far end of the main street, Hazen and a couple of the Jayhawkers stood with three strangers, looking out across the wagon field, pointing now and then as they talked.

I rode to the livery, put the Morgan in his stall, rubbed him down and shoveled some good corn into the box. As I left the barn Hazen and the others were approaching, walking back toward the main part of town.

Hazen saw me and waved a friendly hand, then herded his companions over to where I was and performed introductions. The settlers I already knew. The largest of the three newcomers was a wide-shouldered, full-bearded man wearing a black frock coat and a flat-crowned hat. The hand he offered was a no-nonsense hand, square and hard-palmed. The second was a sleek, dark-haired gentleman in a suit that would have paid for ten outfits like the best I ever had. He was friendly enough on the surface, but I got the feeling this was one who couldn't be judged from the surface. Whatever he was, he didn't share.

The third man was an Indian, though Hazen introduced him just like white people, and he answered in English as good as mine—maybe better. His name was Billy Hawk, and he looked it. Copper and wiry, he wore buckskins and a tall silk hat from which hung long, black braids. He had a face like the bird he was named for.

"Mr. Burnett has been telling me about you, Burke," the big one said. "We're heading for the nearest hot coffee. Will you join us?"

His name was Mason Chapman, and he would boss the train to Kansas. For a fact, he looked as though he could, and twice that far if need be. The middle one was Mark Hayden, who was the Harmony Land Company.

We pulled up around a long table in French Charley's place, the settlement leaders around one end, the Jayhawk farmers and Hazen and me down from them.

Mason Chapman blew into his cupped hands to warm them. "I guess we're ready to travel, in maybe two days."

Hayden tossed him an ironic glance. "You're worrying, Mason. Still concerned about a haul this early in the year?"

He shrugged. "Yeah, but this is when you wanted to go. Be better if we waited out the spring thaws. Easy run from May on."

Hayden smiled coolly and nodded. "That's all been decided, Mr. Chapman. We are going now, and you are going to take us through. Without trouble." The emphasis on the last words spoke of previous disagreement between the two, and of a condescending attitude which the victor had adopted. If it rankled Chapman any he didn't show it. He just wrapped his hands around his coffee mug and gazed into it. "Happen a man was looking to get there ahead of the Free State elections, this is a good time. No other way."

"Look at it this way," Hayden pushed. "The people we have are so land hungry they'd tackle a Kiowa war party for a few acres of prairie. Do you think they could be convinced to wait another two or three months? Past planting time?"

"So what is the schedule?" one of the farmers interrupted.

"If we're bound to go now, then the sooner the better," Chapman allowed. "Two days to pack and line, then we best move. Need to get past the big river while there's ice, after the spring thaws swell her."

"Still figuring to cross at Hannibal?"

"I reckon. It's either there or swing down to Louisiana town, and that's a poor crossing in winter. No islands for staging."

I had noticed that Hazen kept glancing at the Indian, Billy Hawk, with an odd expression, but he said nothing to him.

"We'll make the flood bottoms all right," Chapman said. "But that is the easy part. The worst is the other side of the river. That's Missouri over there, and these are Jayhawkers we're taking through."

Hayden chuckled at the worry in his wagon boss. "Don't fret the thought, Mr. Chapman. That's what Mr. Burnett is with us for. Right, Mr. Burnett?"

Hazen reflected none of the jovial tone in his answer. He was cold and serious as he nodded and said, "That is what I am for."

One of the farmers, the one sitting across from me, pointed out, "We'll be in bushwhacker country from here on, Mr. Hayden. Did you hear about the shooting we had right here the other day?"

Chapman was startled. "Here? Not Missourians, certainly?"

Hazen nodded. "It raises a point, Mr. Chapman. It is possible that you have misjudged the temper of the Southrens. We were counting on a quiet time in this season of the year. We may need additional help in guarding the train."

Chapman considered it. "Maybe," he said finally. The Indian had finished his coffee, and he turned without a word and went out. Hazen paused to watch him go, then he brought himself back to the subject. "What we had here was a handful of renegades. The real hard cases won't be organized this early. I figure if there's big trouble with the bushwhackers it will be at the other end. Beyond Hannibal or later, somewhere in Missouri.

"And as for additional guns," he said pausing and looking squarely at me, "I have a suggestion."

Chapman looked at him thoughtfully. Hayden did the same, then at me, and suddenly showed worried recognition. "You're the one. The man with the Walker gun, that was you?"

Burnett answered before I could. "That was him, Hayden, and the slickest hand with a big gun I ever ran across." He turned to me again. "How about it, Jeremy? Want to go to Kansas?"

I had seen it coming and was already starting to shake my head when Chapman cut in, decisively, "I can pay a hundred dollars, Mr. Burke. One hundred dollars to ride to Kansas with that train out there . . . and another hundred if you stay on a month at the new settlement."

I stopped shaking my head. I was going west anyway. I could do what I set out to do and get paid for it. There were things I didn't like about the way this wagon train stacked up, but that was their business, not mine. I nodded. "I'll think on it, at least."

"It's settled then." Chapman's smile indicated finality.

Hazen was still pondering something, and now he asked the wagon master, "Mason, your Indian, Billy Hawk, I know him from somewhere. Who is he?"

Chapman said, "You might have run across him. Real name is William Hawthorne, but he goes by Billy Hawk. He's a Delaware, and the best man on a trail I ever seen, for a fact."

Hazen shook his head. The name meant nothing to him. "No, but I seem to know him." He looked even more puzzled. "It's like I'd seen him, but he was somebody else entirely. Well, I expect I'll recollect sooner or later."

I was getting up to leave the table when Artemis Steen came bustling in, his nose and cheeks red with the cold, myopic eyes intent. He went straight to Chapman and straight to the point.

"Mr. Chapman, I represent the *New York Tribune*. I have a surrey and two good horses and I, ah, intend to go west to the Kansas lands. I wish to travel with your train."

Out in the street the movers were bustling about, getting themselves supplied, organized, reorganized, and ready for the trip ahead of them.

I was thinking about Chapman's offer, and it dawned on me that it was a chance to shake the Suttons off my track for good . . . or at least for a time. I might just drop off the face of the world where they were concerned. If I could lay a track down toward St. Louis, then double back and meet the wagon train at the river . . .

I was putting it together in my mind when I rounded a corner and saw a ghost, and it stopped me dead in my tracks.

Joshua Sutton had been much on my mind of late, and Suttons in general. But not this one. Back there in Indiana, on a cold graveyard hill, I had shot Joey Sutton dead, and later I had seen him buried.

Now my spine chilled in me like the chill of the day. At a hitchrail in front of the Elmira Hotel Joey Sutton was getting down from his horse.

CHAPTER SIX

It was, as far as I could see, Joey Sutton alive and well. But I knew Joey Sutton was dead. Three .44 balls had gone into his chest in a space you could have covered with a pocket watch.

A cold unlike the chill of the day seeped through my bones and froze me where I stood. The rider's back was to me, but there was no doubt.

The horse was Joey's horse, a little dapple grey with a splinter scar along its rump. The rider was slim and slight, like Joey, with dark brown hair to the shoulders. Like Joey. It was Joey's old brown hat with the eagle feather in the band. It was Joey's heavy greatcoat, and Joey's mulehide boots. Even the rifle crooked across the left arm was Joey's battered repeating rifle, right down to the initials carved wide on the stock. The rifle Joey had shot Pa with, there in the graveyard. All of that came to me in an instant, in the unnatural clarity with which the eye registers the unaccountable.

I have never been one to go weak in the knees, but if there had been a bench to sit on right there I would have used it.

He had alighted and was turning to enter the hotel. I faded back into the alcove between building fronts. Ghost or not, that rifle was real.

Twenty feet away I heard bootsteps, then the creak and slam of the hotel door, and I chanced another look that way. The horse stood there, head down at the hitchrack. I tried to spot my error but there was no error. It was Joey's horse. The hotel door creaked again and I backed into the alcove, then peered out in time to see the rider's back again as he mounted up and turned upstreet away from me.

When he rounded the corner a block away I went into the hotel. The clerk at the desk looked up, nearsightedly.

"That young fellow that just came in here . . ."

"Yes, sir?"

"What did he want?"

"Why," the man hesitated, "he was looking for you, Mr. Burke. I sent him to inquire at the constable's office." There was a cold sweat on my face and the clerk peered at me closely. "Are you all right?"

"I'm all right," I told him. "Ah . . . was he? All right, I mean? Anything wrong with him?"

The man was confused. "Why, not that I noticed, no. Little strange, though, come to mention it. Something, ah . . ." He shrugged. I headed for the constable's office.

As I rounded the corner I saw Hazen crossing the street, opening the door, going in. The grey was outside the office, again standing head down and tired out at the hitchrail. It had come a far piece in a hurry. The doorpane was frosted nearly across but was thawing out in the middle, and I could see Joey's back in there. He was standing near the door, and Hazen was over by the stove taking off his coat. The constable was out somewhere.

Well, ghost or no, there was one thing I could do.

I went through that door like my tail was afire, slammed a shoulder into the ghost, grabbed the rifle away with the same motion, then drew back to see what happened next.

The specter of Joey Sutton did a cartwheel across the constable's desk and landed sprawling on the other side, then let out a high-pitched cry of rage and scrambled up, eyes blazing, slouch hat toppling off onto the floor. And with the hat gone it wasn't Joey at all. But it was sure enough a Sutton.

She was sputtering and fuming and all I could think of to say was, "Oh, hi, Jenny. What are you doing here?"

Well, that took the kinks out of her tongue. She got her wind and yelled, "Jeremy Burke, you are the clumsiest, rudest man I ever had the disaster of running into! . . ." Then she stopped, rushed around the desk, and threw both arms around me. "Oh, Jeremy, you're alive! Thank God you're still alive."

Hazen was standing there by the stove, his coat half off and his mouth hanging like somebody had left it open and gone to town. I looked at him and he looked at me and didn't either of us know what was going on.

Jenny Sutton backed off a half step, her hands still on my arms, and beamed at me. Then her face turned grave. She said, "Jeremy, we've got to get you away from here. Joshua, he's after you. He'll be coming here for you."

"Jenny, Joshua's been here. I saw him."

Shadows swept across her eyes for a moment. "He wasn't . . . you didn't? . . ."

"No, Jenny. He's all right, but I don't know where he is now."

She looked relieved and confused. "I heard about a shooting here, when I came through Danville. I thought Joshua had . . . and then when I saw you and you said you had seen him, I thought . . ." She was starting to babble.

68

Something else was just beginning to dawn on me, too. I said, a little critically I suppose, "Jenny, you're wearing pants."

At least it got her talking straight again. "Of course I'm wearing pants, doggone it! How the blazes you expect I'd ride across two hundred miles all alone? In petticoats and crinoline?"

Her chin went up and she turned abruptly away from me. She raised an oddly ladylike hand to Hazen. "This oaf isn't going to introduce us, I suppose. My name is Jennifer Sutton."

You know how little trivial things can surprise you sometimes? I had never known, or thought about it, that Jenny Sutton's name was Jennifer.

Hazen, always the smooth one, was up to it. Without a pause he accepted her hand in his, gave her an elegant smile, and bowed from the waist.

"A great pleasure, Miss Sutton. I am Hazen Burnett, at your service. Would you care for coffee?"

She smiled sweetly and went to sit in the constable's chair. As Hazen picked up some cups he gave me a sideling glance and an undertone comment, "Real positive way you've got with women, there, Jeremy. Knock 'em right off their feet every time."

Now just the thought of that snip of a girl putting on man's clothes and riding all alone across western Indiana and half of Illinois, through some rough country and rougher men, was enough to set my teeth on edge. Even considering that this was Jenny Sutton, who grew up in a family of men and could ride and shoot as well as most of them, it still did not set right.

But it was done. She was here, and my problems were about doubled as a result.

We drank our coffee and it did take the edge off the shakes I had inside me, first from seeing Joey's ghost and then from seeing Jenny—in the flesh, so to speak. Those baggy britches she had on were poor camouflage up close. Jenny had changed some in the years since her tomboy times.

She had figured out how things were not long after I left home, when Joshua turned up missing. She had gone over to our place and talked to Harley and the girls. Then she had gone back home and confronted her pa, and he had just set his teeth and nodded. "Joshua's doin' what needs doin'," was what he told her.

"Well," she told me now, "your sister told me about the promise you made your father. So I couldn't just stay there and let Joshua find you, could I? I know Joshua as well as you do, Jeremy. Better." She turned to Hazen and explained, just straight-out, "My brother is rotten."

He was standing there taking it all in.

"Anyway," she continued, "when Sonny left, too, I couldn't take it anymore so I put on some of Joey's old clothes and saddled the dapple and here I am."

"What do you mean, 'when Sonny left'?"

"Why, that's what I'm trying to tell you, Jeremy. Sonny's out somewhere, too. I don't know where he is."

Sonny Sutton. Silent young Abraham. Self-contained and deadly with a handgun. As if Joshua wasn't enough.

"So you're here," I said. "Now what?"

She lowered her eyes, troubled. "I don't rightly know, Jeremy. But don't you see, I got to help."

Hazen looked at me, a mixture of disbelief and confusion there in his eyes. "Do I understand that if one of this young lady's brothers was shooting at you, you wouldn't shoot back?"

"Reckon not. I made a promise to my pa."

"But your father is dead. You can't hold to a promise like that."

"Makes no difference, Hazen. It was a pledge."

He shook his head and reached for the coffee pot. "Hoosiers," he said to nobody in particular.

"The first thing to do," I told Jenny with all the authority I could muster, "is to get you back home. You got no business at all out running around in men's clothes."

Her dark eyes went fierce again, and I was a little amazed at how she had grown since those days when she was tagging after her brothers and me back home. "No such thing, Jeremy Burke! I am not going home, I am going with you."

"That," I allowed, "is out of the question. Jenny, I can take care of myself a lot easier than I can take care of you. Now, did you bring some decent clothes with you? Good. There's a coach east from here, through Veedersburg, next day or so. The driver can tie the dapple on behind. When you get to Veedersburg, the station folks there can send to Burnham for somebody to come and get you."

I thought she was going to flare up again, but she didn't. She just lowered her eyes and said, "I'm hungry, Jeremy."

There were several things to do. First, I laid the law down about those pants. She didn't argue any, just sent me out to get the saddle pack off the dapple horse. I had a funny feeling that I hadn't won any argument, though.

I brought the pack in, then Hazen and I went outside and stood by the door and when the constable came along, red-nosed and blowing puffs of steam with every breath, we didn't let him in.

"There's a lady in there," Hazen told him.

"Changing clothes," I explained.

"Oh," he said, and the three of us lined up there with our backs to the door, sort of standing sentry. Old Lucas McCambridge, the town's most punctual stumbling drunk, came reeling along the street and veered over our way to stand with us, shoulders up and chin high. He hadn't the vaguest idea what we were doing there, but old Lucas always liked to do his share.

I had known little Jenny Sutton ever since she was old enough to start tagging around after her brothers back home. But when that jail office door opened and she came out in a dark blue dress with white ruffles around the throat, with her hair done up in back and a silly little hat on her head, I guess that's the first time I ever saw Miss Jennifer Sutton.

She certainly didn't look like her brother Joey anymore.

I introduced her to the constable, then picked up the dapple's reins and we headed off down the street to find her and the horse a bite to eat and a place to sleep.

When we came to the corner, where wagon wheels had chopped slushy holes in the hard surface of the street, she put her hand on the crook of my elbow and hoisted the hem of her dress to step across. And as we reached the other side Eleanor Puckett was standing there watching us.

She had a bundle of something under her arm, and was wearing a checkered gingham dress that fit her something wonderful where the grey shawl let it show. A little bonnet framed her blond curls and blue eyes.

Now since the trouble in town, and maybe since the evening I'd got myself a new pair of britches from that fighting drunk, I hadn't had so much as a howdy-do from Miss Puckett. She couldn't see me for mud. But now, for no reason at all, she stood there until Jenny and I came up to her, then she said, "How do, Mr. Burke. Beautiful day, isn't it?" And while I was getting my hat off my head she gave me a smile that was all sunshine, then turned away with a whirl of bright skirts and walked off down the street.

Mules are a whole lot easier to understand.

All the rest of the way to the hotel, I thought Jenny was going to get a crick in her back the way she was walking.

I got Jenny registered in at the hotel, put her saddle pack in her room, then left her there while I took the dapple down to the stable where I was keeping the Morgan. That poor little grey horse was ridden down pretty bad, but a good rubdown and plenty of oats and grain would set him up all right.

When I got back to the hotel I picked up Jenny and we went over to the Acme for steak and beans.

She was a little cool since running into Miss Puckett, but she had something worrying her, too. While we were eating she said, "I told you Sonny had left home, didn't I?"

"Yes."

"I don't know where he went, Jeremy."

It seemed to have a lot more importance than the words indicated.

A little later she said, "Did you know that Joshua is afraid of Sonny?"

I told her no, I hadn't known that.

"Well, he is. I think even Pa is a little afraid of him."

Then we talked about other things, but I knew what she had told me. Watch out for Sonny Sutton.

Tell the truth, I was more concerned now about

Joshua Sutton. I had seen him, right here in Springfield, just a few days ago. He had tried to shoot my head off, as a matter of fact. Then he had just disappeared. Joshua was an abrupt man, and not one given to patience. But neither had I known him to turn back once he set out to do something.

After I took Jenny back to the hotel, I checked in with the constable again and he had a job for me. Some of the politicians in town, Mr. Jeffries, Mr. Lincoln, Mr. Lewis, and some others were having a meeting over at the town hall, and I was to stand by the door while they were there.

When that meeting finally broke up and I'd walked a couple of them to their coaches, it was after ten o'clock and there was a fine frosty moon lighting the streets and roofs of the town. I decided to check in on the horses before I headed home to Mrs. Walsh's house to get some sleep.

CHAPTER SEVEN

It was one of those nights when the world looks like silver coins under clear spring water. The air was so brittle with cold and so sharp with moonlight that every little sound carried clean across town.

Under slanted roofs the town was a shadow world, bright where the moon hit patches of lingering snow, black where there was no snow, and blacker still in shadowed corners and under the eaves of buildings. It was a night when every breath hung there before you in a little cloud of frost, then shrugged away when you walked on through it.

Here and there pale yellow light fell from a window onto the crusted ground outside. Up the street behind me I could hear the muddle of voices coming from the taverns, and ahead the sounds of grazing animals, out in the wagon train's stock field, drifted clear and calm all the way back into town.

Far out there a dog barked and I could hear it clearly.

It was cold, right enough, a clean, dry cold. I pulled my sheepskin coat a little tighter and walked on past the emporium, past the saddler's dark shop, heading toward the little splash of warm light where the stable lantern glowed through a partly open door.

The alleyway was dark as the inside of a cold boot, and I was at it before I heard a shuffling sound, a barely noticeable sound that made the hair rise up on my neck. It was right there by me, and with it came the sound of caught breath, like a man swinging an axe or raising a cable will make.

It was pure instinct and reflex that turned me half around, and then something hit me in the shoulder and burned like sin.

You'll hear tell that a knife cut doesn't hurt until later, and they'll say that a straight cut with a sharp blade, with the grain of the muscle, won't slow a man down. Don't ever believe either of those stories. When cold steel gets past your skin it hurts like all hell, and it hurts right away.

If I hadn't turned when I did, that long knife would have slid in right next to my spine, just above the heart. As it was, I took it in the left shoulder, straight in under the main muscle and out through the skin above my shoulder blade.

My whole arm seared with the pain of it, then just went numb and dead on me, and I felt the tingle of shock going up my neck. I was turning when it hit, and instinct made me spin right on around. As I did, the wrench of my twist pulled the knife out of his hand.

He laughed, and I looked right into the grinning face of Joshua Sutton. Another man was beside him. Just past them in the shadows was somebody else. Joshua grinned at me like he was the cat and I was the mouse, and stepped back. The fellow beside him went for a sidearm and it seemed like I was frozen, like we were at the bottom of a molasses jug, and I was watching his hand go down for that gun. It wasn't like that, of course, but it seemed like he was moving slow and I wasn't moving at all. I watched his fingers go around the gun butt, and saw the barrel skim upward, even how the front bead nicked at the edge of his belt as it came across it.

Then I told myself, from way back in the back of my head, come on now, Jeremy, you really ought to be doing something about all this. So with that thought in mind I got the fingers of my right hand up tight into the palm, crossed my thumb over them and brought the whole mess up from about the knee. I caught him right on the chin, and lifted his heels an inch off the ground.

Now that all sounds ridiculous, but that is just how it seemed. Actually it all happened in an instant, but it seemed like it took half the night to get to that point.

Then I got my head back in charge again. As the knuckle-dusted one tipped backward, the fellow back in the shadows raised his pistol, moonlight caught the end of it, and I ducked to the side. The powder flash from that gun lit up the whole area for an instant.

But an instant was all there was to go. I didn't have to think on dragging out the Walker pistol. It was already out, and stabbing fire right back down the trail of the pistol flash. A shot, crashing loud in the narrow alley, thumb the hammer, and another shot while he was still feeling the first one.

I was swinging the muzzle toward where Joshua Sutton crouched when my thinking caught up with me. I let the big gun off cock and put it back where it belonged, then braced to take Joshua's rush. But he backed off, dodged between buildings and was gone. The one I had hit was mostly in shadow, just his feet out in the white moonlight, one boot toe sticking up, one turned to the side. I must have stood there two or three seconds before I realized he wasn't moving any.

Somebody was shouting up the street, and a couple of doors slammed. Then there was more shouting. I dug around in my pocket and found a match, then walked over to the man. I lit the match on the sole of his boot and held it high. He was sprawled out on the frozen ground, his gun still in his hand, flat on his back but with his head upright, resting against the six-inch rise of a rock-slab riser, at the edge of the freight office porch.

I thought, now mister, come on. Nobody can bend his neck that way.

Footsteps and lantern light came around the corner with a rush, and all of a sudden the alley was crowded with people. I backed off out of the way, and several of them bent over the two men. In the lantern light I could see the gunman's face. It was the dandy with the dueling irons. Hooper.

Some of the men were telling each other how dead the two on the ground were, and some of them were looking me over like I was a side of beef.

A little wide man with a lantern said, "You all right, mister . . ." Then his eyes got wide and he said, "Jeeze, man, did you know you got a bowie knife stickin' all the way through you?"

Now that was no kind of a joke to make, and I was aiming to tell him so. But I couldn't get my jaws to working. So I just grinned at him and turned away. And fell flat on my face.

The way it is in stories, if you wake up dead you're supposed to see angels in white gowns dancing around and playing fiddles or something. And if you wake up alive you're supposed to find sunlight streaming in through the window and the good, decent faces of your loved ones gathered around you, fretting.

All I got out of it was the sunlight. There was a face there, but it was no loved one. It was Mrs.

Walsh, scowling at me like I'd forgot to pay the room rent.

My whole left arm felt like a carbuncle with fingers.

"You're awake," she pointed out, about the time I noticed that I was. "You bled all over my clean linens," she added.

"It's my room."

"It's my linens. How long are you planning to stay on, Mr. Burke?"

When she finally left I sat up and started to reach for my clothes, draped over a chair near the bed, but I got so dizzy I had to lie down again for a while. And the next thing I knew Hazen was there with Dr. Hollister and a couple of other men.

The doctor was just closing up his war bag, and there was a fresh bandage around my shoulder, wrapped so it went clear across my chest and down my left arm halfway to the elbow. I'd just dozed off a little, and he'd done all that before I woke up.

When he saw my eyes were open he nodded.

"Feeling better?"

"Than what?" I was feeling a little cranky, as a matter of fact.

"You're better," he allowed. "You lost some blood. I'm telling Mrs. Walsh to bring up hot broth for you, and then a rare steak." He clamped his hat on his head. "Drink plenty of coffee, too. Good for you. Come by my office when you're up, and pay your bill. Good day."

Hazen was tipped back in a chair over by the far wall, and the other two were standing by the door, hats in their hands.

"These gentlemen carried you up here last night, Jeremy. They came by to see if you're all right."

"I'm all right. I just can't stand up for goin' to

sleep is all."

One of the men was Ross O'Dell, the fellow I had educated about rabid bugs and coffee stains. The other was a squat little man by the name of Holcomb. They looked like they wanted to apologize for something. "Thanks," I said. "Obliged to you for that. You still sore at me, O'Dell?"

He lowered his head. "Reckon not. That teamster was bigger than I thought, after I looked him over sober. Guess what you done to me was less than what he would have."

" 'Sides that," Holcomb said, casting an accusing look at O'Dell, "Ross damn near done you in when we carted you up here. You had a belt knife poked clean through your wing, there. And we was wondering about it, so Ross here, he pulled it out of you to take a look at it." They exchanged guilty glances, and he went on, "But when he pulled it out you started leakin' so bad he put it back in again."

My arm was sore enough already. But the thought of it made it hurt even worse.

O'Dell shuffled his feet. "Seemed like the thing to do," he explained. Hazen was turned half away, staring at the wall and grinning like an idiot.

"You boys did all right," he said finally. "Go along now, and on your way downstairs tell Mrs. Walsh to get that broth up here."

The knife wound in my shoulder. Joshua's knife. Joshua.

"Where's Joshua?" I asked when they were gone.

He cocked an eyebrow. "No Joshua there. But there's two dead. Bryce Colby and Hooper. Mister, you are hell in a basket with that big gun once you get started. But there were no holes in Colby. His neck was broken."

"I hit him. He fell."

"And then Hooper opened up on you. Let me show you something, Jeremy." He crossed to the chair where my clothes lay and picked up my hat. It was a pretty good hat, brand new. The one I bought when I first came to Springfield. And there was a hole in the brim, just where it passed my ear. Hazen held it in the window's light, musing over it, then tossed it aside.

"How do you feel?" he asked.

He wasn't talking about my shoulder. "Like I've killed a man," I told him.

"Two men."

"Two." It was funny, I didn't feel any remorse about them at all. They had been nothing alive, they were nothing now. But I didn't kill Joshua. Never a Sutton. Joey . . . but not Joshua. I thought of Pa's stricken face when I held him in my arms up there on that hillside.

"I didn't shoot Joshua Sutton."

Hazen was watching me. "No," he agreed after a little hesitation, "you didn't shoot him."

I sat up, pushing the bed covers aside, and my head swam but it firmed up after a minute.

"Does Jenny know?"

"She knows you're all right. She was here, while you were asleep. She asked the same thing . . . if Joshua was there."

"Joshua is her brother, Hazen. Like Joey was her brother. And he was there and I near killed him, too. I tell you, I feel terrible about it. I really do."

"Well," he said firmly, leaning against the wall, "you have no call to. In fact, Jeremy, you have no right to take any credit on yourself at all for those two, and you know it."

"Credit!"

"All right then, blame. But you're taking blame on yourself like it was credit, and you don't have it coming to you either way. She told me how it was with Joey. And I looked around this morning and saw how it was with them two out there. Now brighten up, damn it. They tried to kill you, and they died trying. If you're not the luckiest cuss in town this morning, Jeremy, you're the next thing to it."

"Those two didn't matter," I told him.

"They always matter." He squared his shoulders and grinned at me again. "Nothing wrong with you some soup and hot cow meat won't fix. Where's that woman with the broth?"

By the middle of the afternoon I was feeling better and up and around, although I wasn't much use for heavy lifting yet.

But I was ready to be up and around, whatever. I had been thinking, hoping I guess, that maybe when the broth came up it would be Eleanor Puckett who brought it. But, as should have been expected, it was only Mrs. Walsh, and her temper hadn't improved in the slightest. And the constable came in right behind her with a notepad in one hand and a couple of newspapers in the other.

He had always been decent enough to me, but now he was distant and reserved. "Come to get your statement about the killin's," he said. "You seen these?" He tossed the newspapers on the bed.

The one on top was this week's issue of the *Springfield Gazette*, Hiram Wilkes II, ed. and pub., hot off the press. The copy galleys were even more ragged than usual on the second page—the front page was all advertising—showing how much trouble Hiram Wilkes, ed. and pub., had gone to to rearrange the page to get last night's events in it.

I was three paragraphs into it before I came to the part that made me catch my breath. I looked up at the stern face of the constable. "What the blazes do they mean, 'Jeremy Burke, noted gunman, thought to be from the wild lands of the Far West.' That's not right."

He shook his head. "That's what I told Hiram. He gave me that." He indicated the other newspaper. It was a Chicago paper, with the upper corners pinned back to page eleven. And there, in a reprint from the *New York Tribune,* pertinent lines underlined with heavy pencil, was a description of the background and present dangerous doings of Jeremy Burke, real name unknown, ". . . latest and most daring of the rising breed of bullet bravados, the epitome of the lethal killer for hire, the mysterious paladin who affects a Walker Colt as his deadly nom d' plume . . ."

"You told me you was from Indiana," the constable said, accusingly.

I seriously considered strangling Artemis Steen.

"Sam, you know this ain't so. Not a bit of truth to it."

"I don't know any such thing. Now look, Jeremy, or whatever your name is, I don't know what's true and what isn't. But I know what I got to do, and that's keep peace in Springfield. It's clear enough to me what happened out there last night, but there are them that's raisin' eyebrows over it, seein' you knew the one that got away from someplace before. And seein' you been seein' his sister, right here in Springfield, and all. And bought her a hotel room, too."

At that the color rose in his face, and I could tell it was already up in mine. I started to say something, then stopped. What the hell, who was going to believe it?

He opened up his notepad, asked some questions, and then wrote down the answers, stubby fingers doing their best to massacre his pencil, his tongue halfway out one side of his mouth. I told it to him, beginning to end, just like it happened, and he got most of that down.

He nodded once, grudgingly. "That does sound right. I checked out Hooper's room over at the Empire House. Colby was a wanted man. Looked like him and the other fellow was hiding out there with Hooper. Waiting for a chance at you, I guess."

When the statement was done he got up to go. "When you're up and around again, you come by the office and sign this, then I'll pay you for the service you done on parade duty.

"And, Jeremy, don't think bad of me, but I guess you better get on out of Springfield soon as you can. No hard feelin's of course, but I got to keep things smooth here."

When I finally managed to get up and get dressed, the first place I went was to the hotel to see Jenny Sutton. She was there and packing, and the coach ticket I'd got her, back to Veedersburg, was there on her dressing table, right next to the washbowl.

She let me in and I stammered around a little, telling her how glad I was Joshua had got away and all. She didn't say much, just kept her eyes down.

"You don't have to worry anymore, at any rate," I finished lamely. "I guess it's all over. He'll have had enough now. Probably on his way home right this minute."

She shook her head. "I just don't know, Jeremy."

"I'll be back this evening to see you on the

coach," I told her.

"All right, Jeremy."

Artemis Steen was waiting for me down in the lobby.

"Ah, there you are, sir," he bubbled, hauling a notepad from his pocket. "I have already filed my copy on, ah, the events of last evening, sir, but I would most appreciate the fine details from you, if you please. I assume they, ah, pursued you for some distance before cornering you there in the alleyway?" And he started writing.

There was so much I wanted to say to him, none of it kind, that my tongue couldn't get ahold of the proper beginning. He scribbled for a moment then said, "Yes. And how many would you say there were all together, including the two you dispatched, sir? My estimate was there must have been at least five, but I was unclear whether the others managed to escape, or whether you let them go by design. Possibly to trail them to their leader or some such? Ah, yes, very good." He was writing again. I just turned and went on out. He seemed to be doing fine all by himself.

I ran the errands I had to run, signed the statement for the constable, picked up my back pay, paid the doctor's fee, then went looking for Mason Chapman. He and Hayden were at Charley's, going over a trace map at one of the back tables. The Indian, Billy Hawk, was standing at the bar.

"Mr. Chapman," I said, and he looked up.

"If that job with the wagon train is still open, sir. . ."

"Of course it is," he said, serious, "That is, if you have put your personal troubles behind you?"

"I have. If the job is still open when you get to the bottoms out there, I'll take it."

"Oh? Not from here?"

"No, sir. I'll meet you there. And I'd consider it a favor if no one but the three of us here—and of course Mr. Burnett—knew that I planned to join you."

He was puzzled for just a moment, then shrugged. "Ah. The episode last night. I heard all about it. How's your shoulder?"

"It'll mend. Are we agreed?"

Chapman inclined his head a fraction. "We are agreed. We will look for you out of Star City."

CHAPTER EIGHT

There are two things a fellow just has to get used to in life: trouble and women. Though, come to think of it, that's only one thing, isn't it. The first is a natural aspect of the second, and the second is a prevalent kind of the first. By the time I rode out of Springfield on a spring-loaded Morgan horse that knew just the pace to make my sore arm ache worse, I'd had enough of the former and more than adequate of the latter.

Two episodes had made up my mind on that final point. First, I happened across Miss Eleanor Puckett on the boardwalk outside the constable's office. I forgot for a second that my left arm wasn't usable and like to killed myself raising my hat. She, in turn, like to broke her neck raising her nose and sailed right on by like she couldn't see me for dirt. Then, later on, I went after that crazy Jenny Sutton to put her on the coach back to Indiana and she was gone. Man at the stage depot said yes, she had been there and cashed in the ticket I had spent good money on for her, and the one at the livery said yes, she had come by and picked up her dapple pony.

It didn't take much to figure out that she had taken my ticket money and decided to go back the way she had come, astride a horse, through some of the roughest country east of Missouri. I thought what a tragedy it would be if she ran into some wild bunch of yayhoos out in those hills that hadn't seen a female for a month. Some of those wild yayhoos were decent enough people in their own way and they deserved a better fate than that.

I was madder than blazes. Some folks just won't hold still and let you do the right thing by them. Pa always said the only sure cures for worms are turpentine and righteous indignation. I didn't need any turpentine. No worm would have come within a mile of me.

It feels a lot better to feel angry than to feel guilty, and that was part of it. I had good cause to be angry. Jenny had turned right around and done what I had made sure she wouldn't ever do again: take off across country alone on horseback. And she was probably wearing pants. It is only human nature to find no fault with any human failing and still not abide inconsistency.

So I packed up, told Mrs. Walsh I just couldn't get my rest in a place where things ran across my bed at night, said a few goodbyes around, saddled the Morgan, and headed out that evening with everything back to normal again—just me and that horse, traveling new country and not looking back.

I headed west, into the setting sun. I had a plan, and it was a good plan, nice and clean and just devious enough to work. Joshua was still out there someplace. And maybe Sonny. I didn't know who might be sniffing along behind me, but I didn't want anybody doing that, so I would lay a false trail and double back. In a few days' time I could ride clear to St. Louis and leave plenty of track, then back up the other side of the big river to Hannibal and not leave enough to notice.

All I had to do was go out about six miles west and turn on the swinghills road, and I'd be on my way. Problem was there is this problem that I have.

Sometimes I can't leave well enough alone. I get started in a good direction and then in light of the perspective there I figure out a better direction, and then a better one yet, and half the time I should have stuck to the first direction after all and left off all that figuring.

Like an old draft horse a fellow used to have back in Indiana. That horse could really think. The problem was all it could think about was its feet. And you could always tell when it was thinking. It would start out just like any other horse, going where it was guided, plodding along just fine, and then it would look down and see its front feet. Then it would look around and see its back feet, and that just sort of boggled its mind . . . all those feet under there, all working in crisscross sequence, and the whole business carrying it right along with a wagon in tow. It never failed.

As soon as that horse realized again that it had feet, it started thinking about those feet and the order they fell in, and which one was supposed to step next. Sometimes it would fall flat down in the road trying to make those feet all work properly, and other times it would just get tangled up and stop dead, with its feet all out of order, and there the poor confused thing would stand.

Mr. Meacham—it was his horse—took to blindfolding that animal. If it couldn't see its feet it never got started thinking, and if it didn't start thinking it got along just fine.

Of course, there was the afternoon that Mr. Meacham dozed off on his wagon bench and he and that blindfolded horse wound up on the front porch of the Polk place, wagon and all.

But the point is once you have a good plan, you should stop puzzling about it and follow it. Trust your first judgment. But not me. I'm just like that idiot horse. I get a good path all laid out and then wander clean off it while I'm concentrating on individual steps.

So when I left Springfield I had a perfectly good plan. And by the time I was two miles out I had improved on it. There was little traffic along this road, but far out ahead of me I saw Corley Epperson riding along, also going west. Corley had hung around Springfield all winter, making up his mind to go over to Star City so he could hang around there next summer. And now he was on his way.

Corley was near enough my size and build that he could pass for me at a distance, although up close he wasn't ever near as much to look at as I was. And he had a middling good horse that, far off and just walking, could pass for mine.

It occurred to me that I really didn't want to go to St. Louis at all, and it would be all right if Corley went for me. It wasn't like he had anything better to do. I stepped up the pace, and closed up to where I could hail him, and he stopped and waited.

We howdied and he asked, "You headin' out too, Mr. Burke?"

"I surely am, Mr. Epperson." I grinned at him and turned to look back up the road toward Springfield. "Looks to me like we're the only smart ones around."

"And how's that?"

I gave him a knowing wink. "Mr. Epperson, you don't have to be innocent with me. I reckon you probably heard about the big strike about the same time I did and decided to get there and get in on it before the word got out, same as me."

Corley Epperson never was the world's brightest mudswamper, but he was shrewd enough right then to hold his tongue and wait for me to spill something he might profit by. He didn't comment, just looked at me in a know-what-you-mean fashion and waited for me to open up. Which I did.

"I figure if we push along we can be in St. Louis inside of four days," I told him, "and get to mining before anybody else shows up. You have a claim picked out yet? I'm thinking about the sandbar on the Missouri side about a mile below town. That's where the big strike is going to be, the way I figure it."

"How do you figure it will be right there, Mr. Burke?"

I gave him another cunning wink and confided in him, "Why, because the first color they panned was on downstream from there. Pearls are a lot like gold, Mr. Epperson. Where you find color, you know the big lode is upstream someplace, and that big old sandbar is just the most likely place to look for it. What you and me ought to do is set up adjoining claims on both ends of it, and start our digs there and work toward the middle. I expect we'd both be rich men inside a month."

"Yeah," he said, "I was thinking sort of like that, but I didn't know you knew about it, too. Understand the color they found was pretty good. Is that the way you heard it?"

"Pretty good!" I whistled. "Why, it's the biggest strike since Cook found Hawaii. Just look at this."

I had a piece of sugar loaf in my saddle pouch, and I reached in and rubbed off a few grains on my finger. It was good white sugar, made from cane. I sidled over close to him, looked all around to make sure no one was spying on us, then opened my hand and let him see. His eyes got bigger and shrewder as he looked.

"That certainly is good color," he said.

"Well, that's all it is," I told him, conspiratorially, "but don't you know there's some real pearls where this came from? How come you don't have your arm slung like mine, Mr. Epperson?"

"Why," he said, "I hadn't thought of it."

"Be a good idea if you did, I think. It's recommended you save your arm if you're going to be chunking oysters. I have some more sacking if you want some."

"Well," he replied, "that's mighty kind of you, Mr. Burke."

He took off his coat and soon we had his arm in a sling just like mine. Then I started admiring his coat.

The upshot of it was a fellow who looked a little like me from a distance, riding a horse that looked a little like mine, wearing my coat and hat and with a sling on his left arm like the one on mine, headed south on the swinghills road that evening on his way to St. Louis to mine pearls, with the understanding that he and I would corner the market. And when he was out of sight I headed on west toward the bottomlands that would lead me to the big river.

My pa always used to tell us, don't ever do any man an intentional disservice.

Of course Pa also said, no man is accountable for the results of another man's greed. I had done old Corley no disservice. He had a better coat on his back than he'd had before, and he'd never seen St. Louis before, either. And I didn't know for a fact that there wasn't a mother lode of prime pearls down there in that river. Then, too, I didn't expect to ever see Corley Epperson again anyway, to find out whether he struck it rich or not.

But if any Suttons happened to be back there on

the trail, I was pretty sure they'd be bound for St. Louis before very long. Ever since pairing up with Corley I had guided my mount carefully to herd Corley through the soft places and keep myself where the tracks would be faint. And the sign was clear where he turned on the swinghills road.

I was proud of the astute move I had made, about the same way that old dray horse in Indiana probably was proud of those first two or three steps it managed before it got its feet out of synchronization.

I made several miles before it got too dark to see, then pulled off the trail a few hundred yards, found a good campsite in a depression surrounded by scrub brush, and settled in for the night. Supper was a strip of jerky and some cold biscuits, the ground was hard with late frost and my arm still hurt when I moved, but I slept better that night than I had in some time. And I woke to the smell of coffee cooking.

For a while, coming out of innocent sleep, that seemed about the naturalest thing in the world, until I focused on the fact that there wasn't anybody here but me to set the coffee going.

When I came out of those soogans it was to confront an Indian in a top hat, squatting by a fresh fire and drinking coffee. He looked me over and said, "You're awake." I expect it was because I was standing there in a half crouch with a Walker Colt revolver in my hand and my blankets flying all over the clearing that he noticed that.

It was Billy Hawk, Mason Chapman's tame Delaware.

"Put your gun away and have some coffee," he said. "If I'd intended you harm you'd have been dead an hour ago."

I asked him bluntly what he was doing there in my camp and he looked at me like I'd lost my good sense. "I'm drinking coffee," he explained.

It was that grey hour of false dawn that comes before morning on a clear day and the air was so sharp and chilly that it crackled. Feeling a little foolish but thoroughly awake I gathered up my bedroll, put on my hat, coat, and boots and found another cup for coffee.

"That was a good move you made back there," the Indian said, "sending 'yourself' off toward St. Louis. Those three following you took the bait. You shouldn't see them for a while."

"Thanks," I said, and blinked. "Those three?"

"Sure. The ones following you. You didn't know about them?"

"Well, I thought there might be one. Maybe two. I didn't think there'd be three."

"Counting me," he said, "there were four. You were a regular Fourth of July parade."

"Who were they?"

"Can't say. I didn't see them close. They weren't together. Could have been two were following you and the other one was following them. But after you swapped coats with Corley and sent him south, they all turned that way."

"You saw all that? I didn't see anybody."

"Of course not. They were quite a ways back. They didn't see you either."

"But you did."

"Sure. I told you, I was following you."

"Why?"

He tossed the dregs out of his cup and poured some more coffee, the steam rising around him in the cold pre-dawn. "I wanted to talk to you."

"About what?"

"I want to know how you stand on Mark Hayden's Kansas settlement."

The coffee had thawed out my thinking processes by now and I was wide awake and cranky. That Indian had followed me, and I didn't know why. And now he was sitting in my camp, big as life, drinking my coffee and asking me things that were none of his affair. I didn't stand any particular way on Mark Hayden's business. I didn't know anything about it except that it was worth a hundred dollars to me to ride with those settlers to Kansas and I didn't have anyplace better to go. But I felt I was being pried into by that dry-talking, educated Delaware and it rubbed me wrong. I told him so, and that made no impression on him at all. So I asked him if he realized how close he had come to getting shot when I woke up and found him in my camp, and that didn't impress him either.

He just asked again, "How do you fit into Mark Hayden's plans?"

"Let's turn that around, then, Billy Hawk. You tell me where you come in."

He didn't seem miffed at all, just breathed another cloud of steam off the surface of his coffee, sipped it and said, "I'm a scout for Mason Chapman. I scout and draw wages. Now how about you?"

I put on a face just as stony as his, which wasn't hard to do in that frosty air. "I'll ride guard for the train. Just like Hazen Burnett. I'll ride along, escort the flock, and draw wages."

"Nothing else?"

"Like what?"

"Like do you know Hayden from before?"

"From before what?"

"From before now."

"Never heard of him." Whatever game he was playing, I felt like I was getting the rhythm of it. I just didn't know what it was all about, was all.

"Luther Fritch, then? Or John Thomas Reazin?"

"Them too," I said nodding.

"Them too what?"

"Them too I don't know either."

"You've used that gun," he said, and I flinched. I didn't like that subject at all. But he pressed on. "You killed three men in Springfield."

"Only one!" I started up, then eased off. "Well, two. But I didn't have any choice. If you know anything at all you know that."

"Papers say you're a gunfighter for hire."

"And that's a lie," I told him, smoldering for sure now.

"You go where there's trouble," he asserted, like it was a fact he'd dug out of a book, and I just stared at him a moment, trying to bore in past those flat, black eyes. For the life of me I couldn't calculate why he was there or what he was after.

"I never hired out to shoot," I told him flatly, "and I never started trouble in my life except a few times back home when there was fightin' needed done and nobody else got around to gettin' on with it. For that matter I never scalped an Indian before, though I'm thinking on it right now.

"And as for going where there's trouble, for the past month now I've been doing my level best to go where trouble isn't. That's still what I'm doing."

It was like talking to a straw dummy, for all the expression he reacted with. But then he shrugged and said, "If you think that, then I guess you don't know Mark Hayden after all, just as you said."

I swore at that. "You saying I might have been

lying to you, mister?"

"I'm saying I guess you didn't." His head came up and he looked around. Then he set down his coffee cup and stood up. "You'll have company," he stated, casually. "See you along the way, Mr. Burke."

He strode a few paces into the tall grass, crouched down, and was gone, just like that. By the time I got to the top of the rise there was just my horse there where I had left him, and the Indian was gone like he'd never been there. Facing east into the top edge of a spanking new sunrise I shouted, "You're welcome for the coffee!"

And an instant later a high-pitched shout answered me from off to the south, toward the trail. Then there was silence, then hoofbeats soft on the crisp ground, and a rider topped the rise, coming toward me.

"Decent of you to holler me, at least," Jenny Sutton said when she rode up. "I'd have gone right on by otherwise, then had to double back again."

"Jenny, what the hell are you doing out here?"

"There's no need for that sort of talk," she said coolly, swinging down. "If you'd had your way I'd have been halfway to St. Louis by now, wouldn't I?"

"That was you following me?"

"Of course not. That was Joshua and Sonny. I was following them. But that isn't you they're following now, Jeremy. Who is it?"

"Just a pearl miner," I told her. "And how did you get back here?"

"Oh, I got to thinking, that road was winding south and you planned on going west, so I decided that wasn't you out there at all, so I came back and picked up this road. I guess they made a mistake.

Can I have some of that coffee? I'm about to freeze."

There's no trick to getting a female to talk. Any little thing will set her off. But getting her to talk sense is something else.

When she was hunkered over the campfire, sipping on my coffee that that stray Indian had cooked, she looked up with big innocent eyes and said, "This is fun, Jeremy. Where are we going next?"

CHAPTER NINE

"I expect you mourn your lost ones, Jeremy," Jenny Sutton said. We were riding westward through the tall-grass plains, a high morning sun casting our long shadows out before us where they danced in the auburn grass. Far off on the western horizon was a trace of grey that would be the tops of trees along a watercourse, or maybe where the river bottoms began.

"I do, and sorely," I told her. "And it will be a long time before the sorrow ebbs."

"Your family has always been so close." Her voice sounded wistful. "It must be especially awful to lose the folks you've shared a closeness with."

I didn't answer, because I didn't know anything to say. She was telling me I had a terrible hurt inside, which I already knew, and figured so did everybody else who had lost kin in the sickness back there that winter. But she was also saying there was something special in my family's loss which, somehow, wasn't in hers. I never in my life met a more changeable person than Jenny Sutton. An hour earlier she had been tongue-lashing me for letting her almost get lost at the swinghills road when I didn't even know she was there and by rights she should not have been. Five minutes after that she had been funning me about how silly my arm looked all bandaged up in a sling. A bit later she had been bawling me out for concerning myself with where she went and what she did, which she pointed out was none of my affair. And a little after that she had been telling me that wherever I went now she was going too, but just as long as she felt like it.

And now, she was worrying over how I felt about the bad times so recently past—or maybe she was worrying about how she felt, instead.

Since I was big enough to straddle a horse without a boost I'd seldom had trouble sorting out what people were thinking from what they were saying. It was an instinct, and it seldom failed me. The exception was Jenny Sutton.

Like one time a few years back when Aaron Sutton and I and Jeb Dykes were fixing to go hunting down in the Plum bottoms and some of the little kids around were fixing to tag along. There were Sammy Dykes, Jeb's kid brother, and Joey and Jenny Sutton, and little Bub Samuels from across the creek. They were all hanging around while we packed up, acting innocent, and I knew right off they intended to follow us when we headed out.

So I lined them all up and told them if I saw sight of any of them between here and Zion Ridge I'd tan their bottoms. Sammy said, "Aw, Jeremy," and Bub Samuels said, "Yes, sir," and Joey just ducked his head and turned away. But it was Jenny, the littlest of all those shirttail urchins, that stood up to me, put her hands on her skinny hips and said, "Jeremy Burke, you ain't our mother," and somehow that struck me so funny that I gave in and, although Jeb and Aaron didn't think much of it, told them that if they'd behave themselves they could ride with us as far as Burton's fence.

So we set out, the three of us trying to balance five squirmy little kids on our horses for near two miles. And we'd no more than got started when that Jenny Sutton, up behind me and hanging onto my belt, leaned over and said to Sammy, "See, I told you I'd get us a horse ride."

That's how Jenny always was. Worse'n a Cherokee. Get yourself covered on the east and sure enough she was attacking from the west.

I'd given up a long time ago trying to figure how her mind worked, and these past years, since she'd started to fill out her form and not look so much like a bones-and-grime little tomboy, she was worse than ever.

She said now, "It bothers me that I don't mourn more, Jeremy. It seems like I ought to feel worse than I do. Oh, I do mourn for Isaac, I guess. He was all right. And I miss Mom, but she's been gone such a long time I really don't remember too well anymore. But . . ."

She stopped and glanced over at me, and I knew she was thinking about another brother that was dead and another that was doing his level best to get one of us dead. But when I opened my mouth she interrupted.

"I know you feel bad about Joey, and you're fretted about Joshua, Jeremy, but that's just the point. I really don't . . . at least not like I guess I should."

"They are your brothers," I said. "And Joey was."

She nodded. "My brothers. But my kin isn't like your kin. I'm sorry Joshua is after you, but I can't worry about him. He's a mean man, Jeremy. I know that just like you do. I don't like him. I never did."

She was silent for a time, and so was I. Then she said, "I guess that's awful, isn't it? But that's how it is. He isn't someone I could mourn if he got himself killed, brother or no. You aren't really afraid of him, either, are you?"

"No. Not Joshua."

"But you feel bad about Joey."

I just nodded, and felt my jaws tighten up. I didn't like to think about that bleak day on cemetery hill. I mourned, all right. Always, down inside, the sorrow was there, and that day was the measure of it.

"I mourned for Joey," she said quietly. "When he took sick and then got well but he wasn't Joey anymore, that's when I mourned for him, because that's when he was gone. After that, he wasn't Joey. He wasn't anybody, just a crazy, wild thing."

"It wasn't Joey that killed your pa, Jeremy. It was that wild thing, and that wasn't my brother."

The way it came out, she was defending Joey to me. But at least that one time, I knew what she was thinking. She was defending me to myself. She was telling me that where she was concerned, I hadn't killed her brother at all. I thought about that a long time as we rode on, the sun climbing higher over our left shoulders and starting to have just a touch of spring in its warmth.

Finally I said, "Thank you, Jenny. It's a nice thing you've done."

And that set us off on a new tangent. She perked up and grinned and said, "Does that mean I can go on west with you?"

"No," I told her flatly, "It does not. I told you before, you haven't my leave to tag along with me. Not for a minute."

"Doesn't matter," she flounced around and sat straight in her saddle. "If I feel like it, I will, anyway."

And that's about where we had started out earlier in the morning. I had flat worn myself out explaining that she couldn't go with me, and she just stood there and asked how was I going to stop her.

My best and final argument was when we got asaddle. I told her flatly that this was where we parted. I was on a running Morgan that could leave anything in six counties behind, and all she had was that short-hocked dapple pony.

"There's been enough foolishness," I told her. "You'd best head east now, because if you follow me you'll not even see my heels inside three miles."

"Then I'll got on west alone," she said, "and when I'm all alone out there a gang of robbers will catch me and have their way with me and I'll die outraged on the prairie."

"They wouldn't dare," I assured her.

"And it will be all your fault, Jeremy Burke."

All of which is why we were here now, riding on west together, instead of me riding on west alone. I just gave up, for a while.

About noon we stopped at a grove and had a bite to eat. Then Jenny said she wanted to sleep an hour or two since she had been riding half the night before. I said fine, go ahead and sleep, I'm leaving. And she said if I went off and left her she'd catch up somewhere along the trail and chuck rocks at my bad arm. So she took her nap and I fretted with the horses until she was damn well ready to move on again.

I did get one concession out of her. She had regular girl clothing in the pack behind her saddle. She was wearing some top parts of it now and when we came to civilization she promised she'd dress decent.

Where we grew up, back in the hills, Jenny had worn britches right along with most of the other little tagalong kids around those parts. But it was pretty obvious that Jenny was no little kid anymore. Propriety is civilization's protective coloration.

Like a woods rabbit that turns white in the winter and hides in the snowed-over brush, people learn early on to dress, think, and act in a manner suitable to their surroundings. It saves a lot of unnecessary trouble. The critter that blends with its background is less apt to have to defend itself than the one that doesn't, and the more vulnerable the critter the better it had to be able to blend.

I knew, even if Jenny didn't, just how vulnerable she was. She should have been home where her pa and Aaron could look after her, but since I couldn't get her sent home, it was up to me to look after her until I could deposit her someplace safe.

In the wilds, alone, she was vulnerable to any tough yayhoo that happened along. There are always folks around with more glands than brains, and honor is a thing you don't count on everybody having. Jenny could ride, shoot, and rassle as well as any boy her size, but a scrawny boy is no match for a man, and Jenny, with her shape showing, would be a temptation to any man who saw her.

And I knew that in civilization she would be even more vulnerable. Where people gather a pretty young girl is always the center of attention. One who can't blend securely into her surroundings will get hurt, either by unscrupulous men or by envious women, and I've never been sure which is the most vicious. Most times, I like critters better.

I knew the kind of trouble Jenny could have by what the sight of her aroused in me. The little tomboy had become a girl, even if she didn't know it.

For myself, I fixed the image of Eleanor Puckett firmly in mind for comparison, and resolved to regard Jenny only as what she most basically was—a nuisance.

By can't-see that evening we were nearing the

line of winter treetops I had been watching all day, and the land was dropping off toward a sizable river. That would be the Illinois ahead of us. Beyond was Star City, and beyond that the bottoms began that would edge down a hard day's ride further to the Mississippi River.

Out of Star City, at a place where trails joined, was where I would meet the Hayden party's wagon train. Eleanor Puckett would be there, and Hazen Burnett. On the other hand, so would Artemis Steen and that spooky Delaware, Billy Hawk. Meeting up would be a mixed blessing.

The trail I had chosen the day after sending Corley Epperson to St. Louis in my place was a back one, angling off from the main road, hardly a trail at all, just a meandering track where the tall grass was a little thin, indicating somebody had used it sometime. Once during the day we passed a farmstead where folks were grubbing out a living from the bleak Illinois plains, and since then we had seen no sign of human presence except the vague trail itself. It was near dark when we topped out over a hollow where a frozen stream meandered and saw another house.

It wasn't much of a place, just a slap-up box house with a slat bin and a couple of outbuildings, and a sod shed out back. Between the bin and the shed was a tumble-fence lot with pigs in it. It was a rough, rundown place in all and I would have avoided it except Jenny was cold and I was sore and we were both tired.

When we pulled up in the yard a dirty man with a lantern and a scattergun came out and said, "Murray?" then held the light up and squinted at us. "Oh, thought you was somebody else. What do you want?"

"We're looking for a meal and a place to sleep the

night," I told him, not liking him right off. "I'll pay."

"We got no room for strangers," he said. "Move on."

Two more came out the door behind him, younger and larger copies of the first one.

"We don't need much," I said. "Just a plate of what's handy and a place to bed." I looked around. "We can sleep in the shed out there if you want."

The man frowned and raised the scattergun barrel about halfway up and said, "You heard me. Move on."

The two younger ones were looking closely at Jenny, and one of them gave the other a furtive dig with an elbow. He said, "We got room, Pa. Might let 'em stay just the night, you think?"

Jenny had pulled up close beside me, and now she leaned closer to say, very low, "Let's go, Jeremy. We'll stop some other place."

"Ain't no other place close," the first son said, grinning like a weasel in a coop. Then he looked me over carefully. Without taking his eyes off me he said, "How 'bout it, Pa? Looks like this feller's in bad shape, arm slung up thataway. Needs his rest, I reckon. There's room in the shed, and this'n," he said pointing at Jenny, "she could sleep in the house."

The other son was grinning too, now. "Coby's right, Pa. We got room."

The old man was looking at my Morgan. He twisted his bearded face in thought.

"Nice animal you got there, mister. Reckon it is a shame not to let you rest your mounts a while . . . and yourselves. You said you'd pay?"

"A dollar," I told him. "That's fair."

Jenny's whisper was urgent. "Jeremy, let's go on." I knew she was worried, but I had ideas of my own. This bunch was a pack of weasels if ever I saw one, but even weasels can be useful. I was calculating quickly on what was going to happen next. The old man liked my horse, the boys liked whatever else I might have including Jenny, and I had jumped right in and offered to pay, which told them all that I had money. My left arm was bandaged up in a sling, and Corley Epperson's old long coat hung down around my hips, hiding the Walker . . . but the coat was loose and could be gotten out of the way in a hurry.

If these folk were peaceable, then so was I. But I knew very well they weren't, and if they weren't I wasn't either. The old man stood there a long minute holding his lantern and his shotgun, then tipped his head.

"Clyde," he said, "step inside and bring out somethin' to welcome these folks." The quick grin that passed between the boys was pure weasel, and then the second one, Clyde, turned and went back into the house. So that was how it was going to be. One thing needed done before he came back out.

"Is it a deal, mister? You'll feed and board us at your house for a dollar?"

"Oh, aye," the older one assured me. "We got us a deal."

"That's fine, then. We accept."

Jenny was fidgeting and fussing now like I had gone out of my head, but I ignored her. I would know in a minute whether I had read this bunch right, and I knew what to do if I had.

And sure enough, Clyde came sidling out of the door again, and when he turned he was bringing up a rifle. When I saw it glint in the lantern light I kicked heels to the Morgan and we went right up onto that porch. The horse's shoulder slammed into Coby and bounced him up against the wall. I swatted Clyde alongside the head with that big Walker Colt, then swung it over and thrust its muzzle right under the old man's nose, hammer back. And while he stood there looking stunned I kicked the scattergun out of his hand. Coby was just then rebounding off the wall and as Clyde sagged in front of him he tripped over his inert brother and went sprawling.

"A deal's a deal, mister," I told the old man. "You'll provide us a meal and a place to sleep, and I'll pay you a dollar. But it looks like I'm going to have to guarantee your hospitality. Things'll be most harmonious if we sleep in the house and you boys sleep out in the shed. Now move back."

I heard Jenny let out an interrupted breath behind me and she exclaimed, "Hot Damn!"

Without looking around I said, "Jenny, your pa would whale you for talking like that. Now you get down and take these fellers' guns if you please, and the lantern."

With Jenny carrying the lantern, Coby carrying Clyde, and the old man carrying an audible grudge, I got them herded out to the shed, trussed them up good at the base of a roof support, and tossed a couple of moldy blankets over them.

"By the way," I asked the patriarch as we turned to leave, "Who is Murray?" He just glared at me.

The inside of the house was a filthy mess. Those men's pigs kept better quarters than they did. But there was passable food, a stove, and some straw where we could pitch our blankets.

While we were eating I told Jenny, "I hope you've learned something this evening, young lady. The world is full of men like that, and you're just a little girl. Now when we get to Star City I think you ought to let me put you on a coach heading back home."

She didn't have anything to say to that, but her eyes were the size of dollars in the lamplight and her cheeks were pale enough that the little bridge of freckles across her nose stood out clearly.

After I had Jenny bedded down near the front wall I put out the lantern, wrapped up in a blanket, and sat down in a tipped-back chair by the door. Our hosts had been expecting somebody named Murray.

It was an hour or more later that I heard footfalls of a horse coming in from behind the house.

I have always been curious by nature, a trait that Pa always encouraged. Ma would sometimes say, "Curiosity killed the cat," and Pa would usually answer something like, "If he wasn't curious he'd have starved to death," or, "Indifference would have got him quicker."

A fox hunkered under a stump looks less like a fox than anything else around. The way to collect fox pelts isn't to go poking into places that look like there's a fox there, but to get curious about the places that look like there isn't. That doesn't have anything to do with what I'm telling you about, but it does make good sense. Pa always was curious about facts and folks, and he found a lot of answers in his books. I inherited his curiosity, but found I could find out more by letting folks do what they'd set out to do, and then watching.

I couldn't think of any good reason why this Murray should be showing up way out here in the prairie late at night, so I was curious.

I have noted that coincidence is a powerful force in life. The only thing coincidental about coincidence is that there is so much of it. Anything that happens once is likely to happen again. Anyone you hear of once you're likely to hear of again. And anything you know about you'll learn more about in the most unlikely places.

So it was then. When I heard the rider coming in I got up, and while he was coming around the house I lit the lantern, turned the wick low, opened the front door, hung the lantern on a peg outside, and stepped back into the shadows inside.

As soon as I saw him in the dim glow I said, just like the old man had earlier, "Murray?"

Out in the yard he pulled up and peered at the open door. Then he said, "Yeah, it's me. You boys want some work, Jake?"

He was a big, wide-looking man with a beard that gleamed red in the lamplight. Trying to keep my voice muffled and sleepy, I called back, "Sure, what you got?"

Apparently it satisfied him. He swung down from his horse, talking as he did. "Hayden's bringing a bunch through, be at the river two days from now. It's set up over in Missouri, but Chapman's taken on two gun guards and they'll be in the way."

He had his back to me, loosing the cinches on his mount. "One is that Hazen Burnett, the other's some fellow meeting them down in the bottoms. Name of Burke. You'll know him, he got his arm hurt in a knifing."

He paused to lift the saddle off his mount, and I grunted something to keep him talking.

"You fellows take them two out between Star City and the big river, there's fifty apiece in it." He turned, hoisting his saddle, and stopped, suddenly wary. "Jake? Come out where I can see you."

The bunch in the shed must have woke up about then, because one of them hollered and Murray swung half around, dropped his saddle, and reached for a handgun stuck in his belt. I thumbed back the hammer on the Walker and stepped out.

"Hold right there," I told him, and he did. The muzzle of a Walker revolving gun looks wonderful ominous in dim lamplight.

I added Murray to the crowd in the shed, and when I got back to the house Jenny was waiting there with Joey Sutton's old rifle in her hands. I sent her back to her blankets, then I went to mine, knowing one thing for sure. Somebody was setting me and Hazen up to earn our guard money. I had tried to learn more from Murray, but he wouldn't say anything and when I bounced him around a little it just made him mean, mad, and quieter. I'd need to watch along the way for that one. For a fellow that talked so freely to an empty doorway he surely turned silent under pressure.

Early on a fine, crisp morning, with breakfast under our belts, Jenny and I headed out from Jake's place. I was leading four extra horses, Murray's and three others I'd found in the near pasture, and one of them was carrying a pack. In it were all of those fellows' boots and guns. I tossed an old, rusty kitchen knife into the shed so they could eventually scrape it around to where their hands were, and if they worked at it they could cut themselves loose after a while.

I left a dollar on the doorstep to pay for our lodging, and a pot of coffee making on the stove. It was cold out in that shed and that coffee would taste good to them when they got loose, if it was still hot by then.

Also, I did some swapping. Jenny's old patched-over saddle was in terrible condition, but Murray's was pretty good, so I traded. Jenny needed a better saddle, and a fellow in Murray's business can always find a new one someplace.

Jenny was uncommonly quiet for several miles. We crossed the frozen Illinois River at a place where somebody had bridged to an island, and headed on up the other side of its low, wide valley. We were back up on the plains when I finally turned those extra horses loose. Sooner or later they would find their way back home.

We were near a half day out, angling down toward Star City, when Jenny said, "Those men back there were outlaws, weren't they?"

"No," I told her, "they were church deacons, every one of them."

"They were outlaws," she insisted, her face very grave. "They would have . . . would have . . ."

"That they would, Jenny, and there are lots more like them out here. And over in Missouri, there are outlaws that'll make these look like itinerant choir directors. Soon as we get to Star City, we'll find a safe way to send you home."

I figured that wrapped it up. She had experienced a sample of real life, and that should end the argument. I had a whole minute of feeling right smug about how that had worked out.

Then Jenny said, "Why?"

"Why what?"

"Why do you think I'm ready to go home?"

Sometimes I've wondered whether Jenny Sutton's head works right.

"Because," I explained, "you have now seen what it is like out here in the world, and you realize this is no place for a young girl alone."

She cocked her head at me in a funny, pixieish way, then pulled herself up straight and proud in the saddle. "Don't be silly," she scolded. "I'm not alone, I'm with you."

CHAPTER TEN

Star City put me in mind of Burnham in some ways, though not in others. It was a rough-hewn little road town that stayed alive because it was handy for folks to have it there. The main difference in the places was that Burnham's road went to it, and Star City's road went through it. You could tell that by watching folks in the towns. Anybody in Burnham likely knew everybody else there. Most of the people in Star City were strangers to each other. Maybe a hundred or so people lived in and around the place, but in travel season there might be a thousand more pass through.

It was still a shade early for travel season, but it was getting there, and a lot of the people along the street passed one another by as strangers. It was a jumping-off place, though not a main one. It was out on the edge of civilization, as beyond it were the flood bottoms of the big river and beyond that was Missouri. On past Missouri were the Missouri plains that they were now calling Kansas and Nebraska. Those were the new territories, the new utopia.

And I knew that westward itch that brought folks out here and beyond. I could feel it in my blood, too.

The reason I had left home was mainly to avoid trouble with the Suttons or, barring that, to draw the troubles away from my family. But I knew very well if it hadn't been for that I might have headed west anyway, sooner or later.

I had thought of it enough, and talked of it enough. Pa used to call the feeling "wanderlust," and you could tell from the look in his eyes he understood it. He liked the word "westering," too. Our family, as I understood it from him, had always been a westering family, meaning that in every generation there were some who just couldn't rest for gazing at the sunset and wondering what was out there and yearning to see it. I always supposed, among us children, Willard was the most likely to go westering. But after he and Mary Ann were married he settled in and whatever else was in his mind had given way to taking care of the girl who had come to be his.

Harley never felt it, so far as I know. He was always settled in his way, and he took root right there in the Sugar Creek country and seldom looked beyond. Willard was gone now, and Harley was home where he would always be, and of the boys that left me.

Pa had got us all started reading when we were young, and among the books that I liked were those by Cooper and Blake, that told of how it was out beyond where folks settled, and the journals of Maclamore, about distant trails, seas of grass, great distances open to the soul, and shining mountains beyond.

It had given me a thirst, or sharpened one which had always been there.

There was another book that I read several times because it fascinated me. It was written a long time ago by an Italian named Niccolò Machiavelli, and had been translated into English. It was called *The Prince.* It was about people, a particular type of people who came to be in the places where people settled and intermarried and built a culture around a place. It wasn't about a particular prince, but about princes in general. Princes, I felt, were a product of inbred cultures. Any man so inclined might be a prince, if he had the self-centeredness to desire power, the intelligence to seize it, the ruthlessness to exercise it, and a close, ingrown community to draw it from.

I had turned the phenomenon of princes over in my mind, and compared it to the feel of the frontiers that came from Mr. Cooper's stories, and I had decided that princes were a product of the east, where people buried their fears under the comfort of proximity and traded independence for security.

The west would have no use for princes.

But as each area began to settle, then the princes would come, and some would succeed when the places got old enough and settled-in enough to let them.

It was a disconcerting thought. Maybe some people needed princes to answer to, but I had no use for them at all.

Something about recent events had brought these thoughts back to me, but I couldn't put my finger on just what it was.

As we rode those last few miles toward Star City, just to pass the time, I had talked of some of these things and Jenny listened. I didn't expect her to understand a lot of the spiderweb thinking in my head. She hadn't been raised by my pa, after all. But considering that, she understood a surprising lot of it, and the most surprising thing was I believe she understood about the westering.

We rode into Star City a little past noon of a bright, cold day, Jenny awkwardly sitting sidesaddle to accommodate the long skirt she had put on out in the prairie before we got there, and we found ourselves a meal in the parlor of a rooming house. Then I arranged a sleeping room for Jenny, found a dry stable for the horses and me, and went looking for a bath.

Tomorrow I would meet the wagon train out at the crossing on the river road, and I wanted to look good. Eleanor Puckett would be there.

The fellow at the barber shop looked at me like I was crazy, but for a price he hauled out a big old cider barrel, set it in his back room, brought hot water until it was two-thirds full, and provided me with soap and toweling. I had the place all to myself, since this was off-season for bathing in Star City, and I climbed into that barrel and soaked a winter's worth of sore and weary out of my carcass. One time the barber stuck his head in the door to see if I had drowned.

I unwrapped my left arm in the water, taking it slow and letting the moisture soak the bandage loose from where the front-and-back holes had scabbed over. It was still sore to move, but it was healing, and no trace of infection.

I stayed in that barrel until the water was about the same temperature I was, then I soaped and rinsed, climbed out, toweled off, and was standing there by the stove rewinding my shoulder when the door opened and Mason Chapman's tame Indian walked in.

He looked me over and said, "You're doing that wrong. Wait here." Then he turned and left.

I make it a rule never to be discombobulated twice by the same person, and that Indian had already got to me once, so I just got my boots and britches on and went back to trying to tie up my shoulder. It was awkward and I wasn't doing very well. He came back a minute or two later carrying a roll of muslin and a pot of salve, and I let him tend my arm.

That salve smelled like axle grease and mustard and several other things all mixed up together, and he smeared it on thick, front and back.

"Old Indian remedy," I said.

"Sure," he said. "I got it from a Dutchman at Postoak."

He bandaged my arm and shoulder like he knew what he was doing, and when he was through it was as good a job as the doctor had done before. I pulled on a fresh shirt, strapped on my pistol belt, and hauled out the Walker to check the loads. Then I put it away, picked up my bundle and stepped out into the front room and got the barber to trim my hair and whiskers. Billy Hawk tagged along and stood there watching, not saying anything. When I was fit and the barber was paid I headed back toward that boarding house where they served food, Billy Hawk right at my heels. It was late afternoon now and I was hungry again.

They wouldn't do any more cooking until the evening meal, but there were leftovers from noon and the woman there said I could eat if I wanted. She looked doubtful when an Indian followed me into the place, but she eased up when he took off his hat and sat down at the table just like Christian people. She served us both.

When we had finished off our food she brought us coffee and then left the room. Billy Hawk hadn't said a word all this time, and neither had I, to him. Finally I decided if we were going to keep company this way we might as well be on speaking terms.

"I'm obliged to you for tying my arm," I told

him. "Now, just what the hell is it you're after?"

Those piercing black eyes held mine for a moment.

"I came across a strange thing yesterday," he said. "Place out on the back bend trail, four men had been accosted by a gang of outlaws and left tied up in a shed. Poor fellows had been working half a day to get loose when I got there. Seems those outlaws had run off with their guns, boots, and all but two of their horses."

"All but two?"

"All but two. They'd missed those two, I guess. Those fellows were so riled up they tried to take my horse and rifle."

"So what did you do?" I knew what he was going to say then before he said it.

"Why, I tied them up in the shed again and took their other two horses. I left them a few miles this side of the river, about where you and your friend left the others."

Right then I started liking that Indian better than I had before. He had style.

"I guess you're all right," he said. "One of those fellows was Walt Murray. If you aren't with him then I suppose you're with us."

"And who is 'us'?"

" 'Us' is Mr. Chapman and his wagon party."

"But I already told you that."

"Yes, and now I believe you. You'd better understand," he said, raising a hand for patience, "with a reputation like you have, and no more than I know about you, I had to be sure."

"I don't have any reputation."

"All I know is what I read in the newspaper," he said.

"What you read in the newspaper is hogwash.

Now I'd like to know what this is all about."

About that time the boarding house woman came back in.

"You and your heathen will have to clear out now," she told me. "We got to get ready for supper."

As we stood up Billy Hawk smiled at her, bowed from the waist and said, "Madam, the food was delicious."

The woman looked like she would sink into the floor, she was that embarrassed. Her face turned darker than Billy's and her hands went to her mouth. "Oh, my lands, I never dreamed," she stammered, and Billy bowed again.

"Quite all right, madam," he said with a smile that would have thawed January. "I have some peculiar notions about white people, too."

"Let's go down to the stable, Billy Hawk," I suggested. "We have some talking to do."

Midway down the street Jenny Sutton was coming out of a mercantile store. She had on a new yellow dress, had her hair tied up with a ribbon, and smelled like soap and roses. It took me a minute to know who she was. But when we went on down to the stable to look in on the horses, she went along, and as we talked she listened.

The Hayden party was a day out, moving west on the Newmarket road that cut across several miles south of Star City toward the River Road and the bottomlands beyond. They would stop this night at Rock Ford, and would be at the crossroads late tomorrow for the jump-off toward Missouri and beyond.

William Hawthorne—alias Billy Hawk—had gone on ahead to do some scouting because he was concerned. Mason Chapman, he said, had been in the emigrant business for a while, moving settlers to new lands, first in Minnesota and Iowa, then into the hills beyond the Missouri. I didn't get any idea how long Billy Hawk had been with him.

In recent seasons there was word of a new game being played in the territories that they called land piracy. More than one party past the Illinois prairie had not been heard from again, and no good explanations as to what had become of them. The party had just disappeared somewhere between. The Indian allowed that they might have gone north into the Nebraska plains, or overshot their patent and gone on into the flint hills. But the way he said it I knew he didn't believe it. That wagon train shouldn't have just disappeared like that.

Billy Hawk, I gathered, had some resources of his own, including some contacts he didn't ever mention but had to have had to reach the conclusions he reached. Something was definitely out of whack with the Hayden Land Company. About the time Chapman hired on as wagon master, Billy Hawk joined him as scout and began a little extraneous scouting of his own.

The border lands between Missouri and Kansas were seething. There was open warfare between various bands of Missouri raiders, called Bushwhackers and a few other things, and the Jayhawkers coming into Kansas. There were regular private armies on both sides of several simultaneous disputes in that area, and the term Bleeding Kansas was in common use. Into that cauldron poured a steady stream of people: outlaws, renegades, families looking for homes, freebooters, and decent farmers, the best and the worst of what the settled east could produce.

As could be expected, there were unscrupulous

souls playing the hand for all it was worth. Among these, Billy said, as one particular gang operating in and around the central Missouri hill country. And through his contacts Billy had tied a tough customer named Walt Murray in with that bunch, and then had discovered that Walt Murray had been seen in Illinois, displaying an interest in the Hayden party.

That was why when I showed up out of nowhere and got hired on by Chapman to ride guard, and the newspapers decided I was a notorious gunman, thanks to Artemis Steen, Billy decided to find out just who and what I was.

Walt Murray, it turned out, was the same Murray I had left trussed up in a shed with Jake and his boys. And that had resolved Billy's doubts.

After I mulled all that over I told him what Murray had said that night when he thought I was Jake—about the plans for the wagon train and what Murray had in mind for me and Hazen Burnett along the trail.

"I think it's time we talked to Mr. Chapman," he said.

"And Mr. Hayden?"

"No." He cocked his head and tapped his top hat on a little tighter. "Just Mr. Chapman."

"It's Hayden's land company. It's his party."

"Let's just talk to Mr. Chapman," he said quietly.

Jenny sat on a bale of hay, taking it all in, and Billy Hawk turned a thumb toward her. "What about her?"

"She's going back east," I said.

"I am not," she said.

"Who is she?" Billy Hawk asked, and I realized I hadn't made introductions, so I did it then. Billy gave her his best bow and his thawing grin, and Jenny stood and made a pretty curtsy and said, "Very pleased to meet you, Mr. Hawk. I didn't know who you were when you followed me back there."

He looked blank. "Followed you?"

"Of course. Out of Springfield, don't you remember? You were watching when I turned south. I thought for a while that was where Jeremy was."

"That was you?"

"Yes, certainly. Well, I was dressed for riding, of course."

He looked even blanker. "And you saw me?"

"Well, of course I did. I have eyes, don't I?"

The Indian looked like somebody had swatted him with a wet cloth. I judged Billy Hawk wasn't used to being seen when he was trailing. He glanced at me. "You told her," he said.

"No. I didn't tell her."

At any rate, it was time to do some reasoning with Miss Jennifer Sutton. So I set out to do that.

"Look, Jenny," I said, as sincerely as I knew how. "From here on I've got my work cut out for me. It's been nice having you along, but now you have to go back home. Tomorrow I'll meet Mr. Chapman's party and I'll be with them all the way to Kansas. Nearly three hundred miles. And I don't know where I'll go from there, but wherever it is will be no place for a girl."

She dipped her head and kept her eyes on the ground. She looked so demure, so chastened standing there like that, I had a terrible urge to apologize for having opened my mouth. But I was finally getting through to her and this was no time to modify my position. So I added, "Also, there is no place for you on the wagon train, and you sure couldn't ride along a-horseback, sleeping on the ground with the men, roughing it out there in that wild country. I won't have time to look after you, you know that.

"And besides," I added, coming up with the best coup de grace I knew of where women are concerned, the one that never fails with the fair sex. "What would people think?"

Billy Hawk could have kept his heathen mouth shut right then. He could have stayed out of it. But he didn't. He was still admiring the fact that she had seen him following her.

"There is a widow with two children traveling alone," he said helpfully. "Mrs. Morton. She could use a companion."

I whirled around a stuck a finger practically up his nose.

"You keep out of this," I gritted at him. Then I turned back to Jenny, with all the sternness in my voice that I could manage. "You heard me, Jenny. You can't go. In the morning we'll arrange passage for you back home."

End of discussion. I would have felt a bit easier if she had said something—aye, yes, or go jump in the river, anything—but she didn't, so I let it go at that.

We walked around town for a while, figuratively speaking. Star City takes about three minutes to walk. All of it. But with the day nearing its end we loafed around, seeing whatever sights there were to see. I stopped at the store and bought some powder and beeswax that I was short of, and found out about a family heading east to Springfield in a day or so with a load of sassafras root collected over the winter, and who would welcome Jenny to travel that far with them. Billy and I talked some more about the possibility of a trouble brewing over the wagon party, and added a few details to our thinking.

Then later we got ourselves a bite to eat and I left Jenny at the boarding house to get her rest, while Billy Hawk wandered off somewhere on his own. I stopped in at the local spirit parlor to listen a while, and got started trading tall tales with the old boys hanging around there. Would you believe, not a man among them had heard the one about Willie McBride and his homing chicken? Star City was off the beaten track.

It was late and dark when I got back to the stable. By lantern light I checked on our horses one more time, then spread my bedroll in the hay barn out back and set about getting to sleep. In the morning I would get shed of Jenny, then see what was to be done about those wagon people. And soon I would see Eleanor Puckett again.

That was the note I went to sleep on.

The note I woke up to was an empty stall next to where my Morgan stood. As soon as I saw the dapple pony gone I knew what I'd find at the boarding house. Some people are constitutionally unable to listen to reason and Jenny Sutton is one of them. She had left Star City while I slept. I knew where she would be. And I knew as well as I knew my name that wherever that girl was right now, somewhere south toward the wagon train, she was wearing pants again.

There wasn't anything for me to do but go find some coffee and round up Billy Hawk.

CHAPTER ELEVEN

Seven miles out of Star City the road from there joined the River Road. Two hours' ride south of there that road crested a long swell from the top of which was an unobstructed view of all the land for many miles around. From there in late morning we saw the wagon train, a tiny line of white specks like pearls on a distant string, creeping over a rise in the prairie beyond a distant watercourse, following a westering road that was invisible from where we were, lost in perspective and the tall golden grass. The bright new canvas on those distant bows sparkled white against the muted miles beyond, throwing cold sunshine from their swelling tops. West of them a half-day's crawl, and a couple of hours south of our crest by fast horse, was the crossroads where we would meet, just above the mist of silver treetops that marked the beginning of the floodplains. And off beyond that, within sight although we could not discern it, was the Hannibal crossing on the Mississippi River.

Hannibal, as Billy Hawk described it, was a placid little town on the bluff above the river, linked by the big water to other pockets of civilization above and below but backed up against the barely tamed wilderness that was Missouri. Two hundred miles beyond that point—twenty days by wagon trail or eight days by river—was Westport and the Kansas border. And somewhere beyond that, in a pocket of the Kansas hills, was a valley which was Mark Hayden's patent and was to be the new settlers' home.

Billy figured two days from the River Road crossing to the Hannibal ferry and one more day to get across the river. Then the real journey would begin.

There was much that was odd about the Hayden enterprise. Most such expeditions of the time assembled at St. Louis and traveled by river across Missouri, either to Cutter's Haven or Siloam, and then trailed from there on into Kansas. Those were used routes and some protection could be had from federal marshals patrolling the territory with troops out of Westport. Also, we were early. Most of the travel would begin a month from now and last into the summer.

Mark Hayden said both of these—the cross-country route and the early passage—were to protect the train from the vandals who rode the river in travel season seeking Jayhawkers to devil and loot to steal. By taking little-used routes through wilderness country, he said, we would not be expected or bothered. It seemed to me that would work the other way if our passage were known. There would be a lot of lonely miles out there with no witnesses about.

Billy said Hayden had tried to get full payment in advance from the settlers' party, for the land, the wagons, the supplies, and the arranging of the expedition. The party had voted against that. They paid Hayden for the wagons and supplies, and half the fee for passage. They would pay him the rest and buy their landsteads from him when they arrived there. So, it stood to reason, they were carrying at least that much wealth with them.

Hayden had introduced a man named Luther

Fritch into the party and made him captain, and then brought in the Reverend John Thomas Reazin and named him chaplain. Billy Hawk didn't like any of the three of them. They were, as he said, "thicker than thieves," and he didn't go along with the notion that they had all just met one another while getting up this expedition. Billy felt they had been associated before.

Then Mason Chapman had signed on as wagon master, with Billy as his scout, and had hired Hazen Burnett and me as guards.

"Don't know if you know it," Billy said, "but Mark Hayden didn't care for that turn at all. He said guards would be a waste of money."

"Hayden was there when I hired on."

"Sure, and he didn't object. The running of the train is Mr. Chapman's job. But he didn't like it."

I remembered Mark Hayden's welcoming smile when I had agreed to serve as guard, and I had seen nothing insincere in it. That irritated me now, and I chalked up one small chit against Hayden. I have never liked folks who are as good at misdirection as I am. Of course, I haven't met many.

It was past noon when we came down to the crossroads, where the River Road curved away north and south and the Newmarket road bore in from the east to intersect it. We had not had sight again of the wagon train, but knew they were still hours away at the pace of draft animals.

We lit down, tended our mounts, built a fire, and had ourselves a meal which included three tins of peaches I had paid a price for in Star City. An army deserter had come through three months before and sold a case of them to the storekeeper. Tinned food was rare outside the army and some cities, and he was charging all the traffic would bear. But with the excitement of going west and the prospect of being paid for it, I was feeling generous. Since I was providing the peaches I let Billy Hawk do most of the work. My arm was getting better, but if you have ever tried to off-saddle a skittish horse with one of your arms in a sling, or cut firewood that way or a lot of other things, you take any opportunity not to have to. There had been times the past week or so when I had to cuss and sweat just to buckle my britches. And putting on your boots with only one usable hand, now that is something else again, too. That is one thing Jenny had helped me with, bless her damn fool little heart. My boots, not my britches. Since I was a toddler I had not required assistance with my britches.

"Show me something," Billy said after we had finished eating and were standing under a bare old tree enjoying the hint of spring in the bright air.

"Sure. Like what?"

"Well, what it said in the paper about you being a 'paladin of the pistol,' " he asked.

"Was pure garbage," I said flatly.

"But that thing you carry there," he said pointing at the Walker, "is too big to be either quick or accurate in the hand. I saw you pull it the other morning, and that was fast. I want to see you shoot it."

"Why?"

"Because I'd like to know," he said, and he was serious.

I nodded.

"Over there behind you—no, don't look yet—is a broken stump with a white wood snag on top. It's about thirty yards away, and the size of a man's head. Turn and shoot it, Jeremy. Now."

So I turned and it was there and I shot it. The

Walker thundered and the white snag shattered clean off that old stump. Billy Hawk stood there a minute with his mouth open. Then he said, "Hot Damn!"

"Pistol-witching. That was what my pa called it. This was his gun."

"Did he use it like that?"

"No. Not like that. I don't know where I got that. I just have it."

He nodded. "All right. Now I know."

"Why did you want to know?" I set about swabbing and reloading the Walker. A gun with six chambers should have six loads. Otherwise you might as well have only five chambers.

"Partly that fellow Murray," he said. "I know about him. He's a mean one and you humiliated him back there. He won't rest easy now."

"I'm sure sorry to hear that."

"Don't take him lightly," the Indian said. "We'll have trouble out there somewhere. I feel it. Walt Murray is mixed up in it, and when it comes he'll be there."

"Then I'll face him when I have to," I said with a shrug.

"Not Walt Murray, Jeremy. You can expect him to be behind you. That's his way."

Double, double, Macbeth's witches sang in the Shakespeare play, toil and trouble. And never an end in sight. Joshua Sutton was gone, finally. He and Sonny were off on a false trail to St. Louis following an erstwhile pearl miner, and so far as I knew, Aaron Sutton was still back home. So was I clear and fancy-free? No. I had gone and picked up another enemy to fill the gap and this yayhoo was a back-shooter. I guessed it was another talent I had.

Hazen Burnett rode in just about dusk, and fifteen minutes later the first wagon came in sight. They came rolling in with the evening chill, one after another, and by dark the campsite was a sizable town; those big wagons parked around in every open spot, people bustling about, campfires springing alight, mass confusion that slowly ordered itself into form. It was a city on wheels preparing to rest itself for the night.

Jenny Sutton was driving the fourth wagon in. She had on her new dress and her ribbon, with Joey's old greatcoat thrown over the whole assemblage, and she was sitting up beside a pleasant-faced woman of about thirty. That would be the widow Morton.

I glared at Jenny as they pulled past and she tilted up her nose and ignored me. Then I went looking for Eleanor Puckett. It took me a while to find her. The Puckett wagon had come in on the north while I was looking on the south. I howdied them and set out to help old man Puckett as best I could with unhitching his animals. I had remembered that Eleanor was beautiful. I had sort of forgotten that her attitude toward me was less than friendly. Both were still true. If anything, she was cooler toward me now than when I had last seen her in Springfield, and I couldn't understand that. Certainly she might have been a bit shocked back there, but nothing I had done merited any lingering disapproval so far as I could see.

She was civil enough, but remained totally distant. I had been waiting so long to see her, however, that I bulled right in and tried to get myself invited to supper. She headed that off cleanly. She and her father would sup with another party.

Well, that was no real problem. I said, "Then possibly later, after supper, I might call at your wagon. We could talk for a while."

She looked at me with complete disdain.

"Mr. Burke," she said, "let us understand each other. I do not care for your attentions and would rather not associate with you."

"Miss Puckett," I answered soberly, "I realize you might have been offended by my actions in the past, but let me assure you those incidents were not my doing and I had no choice in what I had to do."

For a second she looked puzzled, and I pressed on, "Whatever judgment you have made about me, Miss Puckett, I submit that you owe me the chance to clear my name in your mind."

She was still puzzled. "I owe you? And why would that be?"

"Because," I said with my best two dollar smile, "of my continuing devotion to you and my determination that you be fully aware of it."

The puzzlement faded, but instead of the tentative smile I had every right to expect at that point I received a frown of pure distaste. "Well," she huffed, "I never!"

"Truly, Miss Puckett, I am not so bad as you seem to have decided. I am an honorable man, after all—"

"Honorable! Mr. Burke, you are insufferable. I suppose I am to be toyed with and then left to fend for myself in the wilderness while you go on to other conquests, is that it? I suppose I am to be enticed away from home and family, forced to remain with you across thousands of miles of hostile wilderness, beaten if I try to steal away, used as meets your whim, and then abandoned without notice. Isn't that how it is done, Mr. Burke?"

She was so angry her cheeks had gone white, and I had not the vaguest idea what she was talking about.

"See here, Miss Puckett," I said, raising a pleading hand.

She backed off a hurried step. "Oh, yes, and you would hit me, wouldn't you? I understand I am not the only lady you have brutally attacked. Good evening to you, Mr. Burke, and please do not have the gall to speak to me, ever again."

With that she turned on her heel and stalked away. Several people were standing around admiring the show, the women glaring at me like I ate babies, the men just curious and interested. I was stumped. At least, for a moment I was. And then some light began to fall into the dark corners as I got it sorted out. I felt my shoulders and jaw muscles bunching up and the blood rushing to my face. Jenny. That damned Jenny. That double-bedamned Jenny Sutton. With teeth gritted so tight I could hardly breathe I turned and bowled full into someone else standing there, sending him sprawling. He lit on his bottom and just sort of froze there, his right hand still sticking out ready to shake, the way it had been when I bumped him. I didn't have time for him right now, so I just said, "Good evening, Mr. Steen," and roared right on past. Behind me I heard a shaken voice.

"Ah, good evening to you, Mr. Burke."

It was fifty yards to the Morton wagon and if I had gone there I guarantee there would have been hell to pay for Jenny Sutton. But I got headed off. Billy Hawk came out of the shadows halfway across, took my arm and said, "I've been looking for you, Jeremy. Come on, we have to talk to Mr. Chapman."

West of the encampment, down in the trees where a trickle of thaw water lapped along the bottom of a run, Mason Chapman and Hazen Burnett were waiting for us. We walked on with them a ways without conversation except when Hazen looked at me curiously and said, "You look like you're ready to whip somebody."

"I'm thinking about it," I told him.

Finally, well out in the brush away from the wagon camp, Mason Chapman turned to us and said, "Let's hear it."

Billy Hawk filled them in on what he had learned and what he suspected, then I told them about my encounter with Walt Murray and Jake and his boys. Hazen interjected questions now and again, but Chapman just listened until I was done. Then he asked me to go over my conversation with Walt Murray again, word for word, the best I could remember it. So I told that part again, how Murray had thought I was Jake, had offered a job of work, and had said Hayden would be bringing a bunch through; how he had said, "It's set up over in Missouri," and then had wanted Jake and the boys to "take us out," Hazen and me, before we got to the river. He had offered fifty apiece. I didn't know whether that was fifty for each of us or fifty for each of them.

When I finished the review he grunted, then turned to Billy.

"You believe that was the same Murray?"

"I know it was. I saw him."

"If they proceed, how soon can they be here?"

"That's a long way to walk barefoot," Billy said. "It's possible they could have regained their horses in a day or so, in which case they'd be two days behind us, about. But we stopped at Star City, and now we've stopped here, and we'll be two days getting through the bottoms down there. They could catch up."

"They might not play it that way now," I said. "They know they've tipped their hand, and we'll be waiting."

Hazen was looking thoughtful. "If I was them," he suggested, scratching his beard, "I believe I'd let us wait. And then after we got through waiting, then I'd come after us."

"Across the river somewhere," Chapman mused.

"Then again," I put in, "if it was me figuring it, I'd figure we'd figure that way and I might go right ahead and do what I figured we'd figured I wouldn't do."

"How's that again?"

"He said they might go right ahead and do it," Billy Hawk explained.

"Or," I continued, "if I wanted to get fancy, I might figure out both of the possibilities we'd expect, including that one, and then do something we just wouldn't count on either way."

Chapman looked at Hazen Burnett. "You told me about him," he said, "and I didn't believe you. Now I do."

"I understand perfectly," Billy Hawk said. "So what would that be that we wouldn't count on either way, Jeremy?"

"Well, the obvious possibilities being either this side of the river or the other side of Hannibal, I guess their place if they're that clever might be either the river itself or right in Hannibal."

Billy turned to Chapman. "He means—"

"I know what he means. I got ears. How smart would you say this Murray is, Billy?"

"Not very, although he is clever, and he's a sneak. I'd say we need to know how smart the man he's working for is."

"But we don't know who that is."

"No."

I was thinking of Billy's penchant for feeling how things were, and I know from experience that hunch-taking is contagious. His hunches when we had talked before had taken root with me and produced some hunches of my own. I wasn't sure, but I was pretty sure. I said, "I have a hypothesis."

"I saw one of those once," Hazen said chuckling, "but I was afraid to go near it."

Chapman glowered at him, then said to me, "What is your hypoth . . . hypoth . . . whatever, what is it?"

"We need to know how smart somebody is without knowing who it is we need to know about. So how's if we hypothesize? How's about we just pick someone . . . say, Mark Hayden for instance . . . and proceed as though it were him we were wondering about. How smart would you say he is?"

It was dark enough I could barely see Chapman's eyes. "Hayden?" he asked. "You think Mark Hayden is? . . ."

Billy backed me on it. "It is possible," he said. "I concur with Mr. Burke's hypothesis, Mr. Chapman."

It's good to converse with an educated man sometimes, even if he is a heathen Indian. I gathered William Hawthorne and I had read some of the same books.

"I think you're all three about half loony," Mason Chapman said. "But the hypoth . . . hypoth . . . the idea might be all right to work with. Let's suppose it were Hayden . . . or somebody like him. He's smart, all right. Now where does that leave us?"

"That leaves Hazen and me getting shot at on the

river or in Hannibal," I said. "Or someplace else."

"And if we're killed then you and the train go on into Missouri without gun guards," Hazen added.

"And somebody has something 'set up' over in Missouri," the Indian said. "But what?"

Chapman was silent for a long time, thinking. Finally he said, "I'm remembering about the Dinsmore party. I don't like this. I don't like it at all. Come on, let's get back to the wagons. We'll talk some more later."

So we had about three hypotheses stacked up on top of each other, and they weren't based on much more than a secondhand hunch. Billy didn't like the Hayden-Fritch-Reazin triumvirate and Mason Chapman didn't like the situation and I didn't like the way Mark Hayden smiled when he was unhappy. And none of us liked the idea of getting shot. So out of all that for whole cloth we had cut a pattern and sewed up a shirt and we were fixing to wear it and see if it fit.

But I'm one who believes in hunches. Pa used to say, "A hunch is wisdom that can't get through the narrow places in the brain. Your head is always smarter than you know how to let it be, so if it tries to tell you something, boy, you listen."

I wasn't happy with the situation, but I was content with the way we had it analyzed, and I guess the others were, too. Until something better came along I for one was willing to assume that our biggest problem was to know just how smart Mark Hayden was.

If that sounds unfair, well, it isn't me that preaches against making judgements of people without really knowing them. You can't ever get to know folks without judging them first, and even when you know all you'll ever know about anybody, you still don't know very much about them, so at what point do you make a valid judgement? I submit that sometimes one glance is all it takes. The difference between a quick judgement and a valid judgement of another might be in how well you know yourself. Chew on that for a while.

The smell of cooking pervaded the cold night air, and I was hungry. I still hadn't had my little chat with Jenny Sutton, and I was still mad enough to spit nails, but I figured if I could temper my temper just a bit I might also get a meal out of our confrontation, so when I walked toward the Morton wagon I was cool and collected. Jenny and the woman there looked up and saw me coming, and Mrs. Morton dipped her head to whisper something to Jenny. Jenny nodded and pointed at me and whispered something back, then they both turned starch-straight backs in my direction that made it clear their campfire was closed to people of my ilk. I could cheerfully have strangled Jenny Sutton then and there.

As I turned away Artemis Steen came from someplace and joined me, bouncing along at my elbow.

"May I ask you a question, Mr. Burke?"

"Sure. Do you want an answer, or have you got your own?"

"It strikes me," he said, unruffled, "that there is an oddity afoot here." No wonder his editor had run him off.

"What would make you think that, Mr. Steen?"

"Ah . . . I'm not sure. Something I have heard . . . I probably have it here." He pulled out a wad of notepads as thick as his fist, and stared at them blankly. "Something, I'm not sure."

I stopped, and so did he.

"But you think there is something wrong?"

"Something . . . ah . . . strange, yes. I must go through these notes."

"Well, I guess I can't help you, Mr. Steen. But I would be curious to know of it if something comes to light."

He turned away, disappointed. "Yes, of course."

As an impulse I asked, "Have you interviewed Mr. Hayden about the wagon party, or Mr. Fritch?"

He looked back, interest in his eyes. "Yes, I believe I have. Possibly I should look through those notes again?"

"It wouldn't hurt," I told him.

There was still the question of supper. I could make out my own if need be, but it would be a lot easier to eat somebody else's cooking. So I wandered through the encampment, getting the lay of the wagons and who seemed to match up with which rig, and ended up at Mason Chapman's battered overlander. He and Hazen Burnett were just beginning to cook a meal. I eased into the firelight and asked, "Mr. Chapman, is my hundred dollars plus keep or including keep?"

He didn't even look up. "I always pay wages and keep."

"Good. Throw on some more meat, then. I'm hungry."

CHAPTER TWELVE

The travel arrangements would be that the crew—which was me, Hazen Burnett, Billy Hawk, and an aging stock-hazer named Willard—would eat from Mason Chapman's supplies unless we could rustle up something better, and we'd all pitch in or take turns with the cooking, all except Willard. Some of the things he cooked nobody else would eat. Mr. Chapman slept in his wagon and if it rained Willard and Billy, being regulars, had first call on pitching their beds under it. Hazen and I could sleep wherever we had a mind to as long as we didn't cause trouble among the party. Ruction, Chapman called it: "I'll have no ruction in any train of mine."

Seems he'd had a line guard one time who got cold sleeping alone so he borrowed some immigrant's daughter to warm his blankets for him. Caused such a ruction that the train disbanded and took off as four separate parties and Chapman never got paid a nickel. He swore when he found out who started the trouble he'd line the fellow up and shoot him on the spot.

"Keep the customers safe," he instructed, "and keep them happy. But that means generally happy, not specifically happy."

He was looking straight at me when he said that. I got stiff-necked about it and he waved off any reply.

"No offense meant," he said. "But I heard a sort

of rumor today, from some of the women."

"I just bet you did."

Billy Hawk and Willard wandered in in time to eat. Willard had been gathering firewood. Billy had been sitting in the bushes watching Mark Hayden's wagon, thinking over our hypothesis.

"I got to go over there after a while," Chapman told us. "Fritch and the Reverend will be there. We'll decide which trail to take from here to the river."

"Is there more than one?" I didn't know this country.

Billy Hawk said, "There are two this time of year, before the river rises. The regular road along the high ground and another one that angles off through the bottoms. It's just an old game trail but herders use it sometimes in low water season because the grass is better."

"Which one will you take?" I asked Chapman.

"I like the road. I'm used to it . . . although this time of year there isn't much difference. Why?"

"Would Mark Hayden know the difference?"

"Don't know why he would. Why?"

"Just thinking. Whichever one you fellows decide on tonight, I think we ought to take the other one tomorrow."

Billy Hawk looked amused. "Matter, Jeremy, don't you trust your own hypothesis?"

"Not 'til I have to. But we might be able to test it. We know the fellows gunning for us won't be ready yet, but chances are whoever hired them won't know it at least before tomorrow."

"That's right," Hazen Burnett chimed in. "I concur with Jeremy's hypothesis about taking the wrong trail."

"That isn't a hypothesis," Billy Hawk corrected him. "That's a diversionary tactic."

Mason Chapman looked slightly dazed. "You're all crazy," he said, shaking his head, "but I'll go along as long as it don't slow us down. Now, I expect to make the high bar by nightfall. I'll want you out ahead, Billy, judging trail, and you gun guards can work back and forth carrying word and keeping lookout."

Billy shrugged, Burnett nodded and I said, "No."

"What do you mean, 'no'?"

"Billy's been watching Hayden and his friends. He ought to be doing that tomorrow when we switch trails. He knows them better than Hazen and I do. One of us can scout trail and the other relay."

"What do we want to watch them for?"

"Just testing a hypothesis. I figure if our hypothetical head man is really him, he'll already know this country or he couldn't have directed an ambush out here. And if he knows the country he'll notice the switch. And if Billy knows him he'll notice that he noticed."

"So what?"

"So if he notices that we're on the wrong trail then that substantiates our hypothesis."

"Partly," Billy Hawk amended.

"I concur with the hypothesis," Hazen said, relishing the sound of such words out of his own mouth.

Chapman pawed at the air like he was swatting mosquitoes.

"It also cuts our chance of getting shot at about in half," I pointed out.

The wagon boss chewed it over. Finally he said, "I'll go along, even if you can't none of you speak plain English. But from here on out, Mr. Burke, let's all remember who runs this train. Me. I'm the wagon master. You're the gun-guard. And being a notorious pistol prodigy don't qualify you to get wagons through on time."

"Now damn it all, Mr. Chapman, I am no such thing!"

"You got to be." He gave me a look of finality. "I read it in the newspaper."

Whenever I got the time, I decided, I would sic Artemis Steen onto Jenny Sutton. That ought to fix both of them.

Across the way, a lantern burned at Steen's covered surrey. The writer was working late on his notes. That was an odd question he'd had about something being wrong here. I hoped he made sense out of whatever was bothering him.

Nearby, in the center of the camp, Mark Hayden's wagon and Luther Fritch's sat side by side, and there was light there, too. Hayden and Fritch had a table and folding stools set between their grounded tongues and were deep in discussion. I had gotten my first good look at Luther Fritch earlier. He was a burly man, the kind that looks fat but usually isn't. And his eyes never stopped moving, flicking one way and another, assessing everything. I took him for a greedy man, at first judgement.

Before we all turned in that evening Billy Hawk filled Hazen and me in on the next couple of days' worth of travel. It wasn't far from here to the river, but it would be slow for the big wagons. After the first mile or so we would be in the flood bottoms, and anything passing for a road down there was barely that if at all. The ground was still hard with frost, but we'd be only about three miles from where we were right now when we made camp on the high bar, which was nothing more than a swell of slightly higher ground paralleling the river midway between here and there.

The distance from here to the big river was either two short days or one very long day. Chapman had chosen the two short jumps to save animals and equipment.

Billy expected the river might still be frozen over but wasn't ready to trust the ice to the weight of heavy wagons. The day after tomorrow, when we arrived there, he would have to be there ahead of us to be able to advise Mr. Chapman on the best procedure for crossing.

Sometime in the cold of winter the ice on the river here was plenty thick to support commerce. But there had been some thawing days of late. He expected we would need barges out of Hannibal to raft our train across. Chapman had anticipated that and had arranged for them in advance.

I went to sleep thinking of that river ahead. Half a mile wide. I could hardly wait to see it.

With the morning bright and cold upon us we got them lined up and moving, all forty-two overland wagons, three supply rigs, one surrey, a hundred and seventy-five-odd head of mixed stock, one hundred and forty-five people, and one Indian. The grade was barely perceptible, but looking back from a little ways along you could see we were going downhill. Once they were started Billy Hawk dropped back toward mid-train where the Hayden wagon rolled high and handsome with four fine riding horses trailing behind. Hayden didn't let his trail stock in with the other stock either at night or on the trail. Hazen Burnett and I moved out ahead, reading the road as Billy had called it, and within a few minutes were out of sight of the train in willows and water brush. From there we kept a keen eye on our surroundings. I really didn't expect Jake and his boys to go ahead with their job after the time I had given them. They didn't strike me as having the salt to put themselves out much. But it didn't hurt to be wary. I didn't know where Walt Murray was but I suspected his place in the scheme of things would be over yonder, somewhere in Missouri, where a surprise was being prepared for the Hayden train, with Mark Hayden himself possibly behind it. At least, that was as good a premise as any for the moment.

A mile out, about where the land began to drop away in little dips and wash bluffs, the trail separated into two. Neither one was any great shakes for a road, but the right-hand one went on down along the receding bottom lands while the left one stuck to a faint rise that angled slightly south. We took the right one, and from here we worked.

Every time we crossed a "nod," one of those little foot-high cliffs where last year's high water had cut away some soil, we got down and smoothed it with spade and root-hoe to the width a wagon would require. Each time we came to heavy brush obscuring the path we cleared it aside. I wasn't much help, with only one good arm. And all along we were watching for seeps and puddles that might bog a wagon. We found none. It was still too cold.

We had worked an hour or more and progressed half a mile when Billy Hawk came riding in from uptrail.

"Your hunch paid off, Jeremy," he said, leaning from his saddle to judge the latest ramp we had scooped. "I just happened to be right alongside Mr. Hayden's wagon when we came to the fork and stayed right. He looked like he'd swallowed a whole egg. Then he turned the lines over to Mr. Fritch and lit out to raise hell with Mr. Chapman."

"I expect you got to where you could listen."

"Sure. Mr. Chapman told him he had decided this would be a better road because there might be snakes on the other one. He wants one of you to come on back now and ride guard. The other one can help me."

I turned toward the horses, but Hazen was ahead of me. As he climbed aboard his sorrel he said, "I'll keep an eye on the customers. You fellers have a good time."

We were at the high bar by noon. It was middle afternoon when the wagons arrived, creaking in across the rough, frozen ground, a lot of the men cross and rough-edged after seven hours of hard work to go less than three miles. Their irritation amused Billy, and Chapman just passed it off. "They're green," he said. "Five days of easy rolling and one day of bottoms don't break them to the trail. Wait'll we get to the breaks this side of Grand River. They'll wish they were back here again."

When the wagons were placed Chapman sent Billy and me on ahead to the river to look at the crossing. Hazen would stay on hand with the wagons. None of us was worried about trouble here in these east bottoms now, but some of the settlers were spooked from being in their first real wilderness and having a gun-guard around pacified them.

We saddled up and lit out, and half an hour later, from a bank it would take the wagons half a day to reach tomorrow, we were looking at the grandest sight I had yet seen.

Hearing about the "big river" is one thing. Seeing it is another. And seeing it then, at the tail end of a hard winter when it was still iced over from bank to bank, was something I was not prepared for.

Where we came out was on a bank in a long bend,

with the iced river curving away toward the south, grey-white and huge under a sky that was clouding over, running on and on until it blended into a horizon of grey mist. Before us was an island, a hundred yards out across the ice, the trees on it skeletal and wispy. Beyond was more river, with the far bank cold and distant. All the snow of weeks ago had gone, but the surface of the river remained solid ice, and that before us, in the lee of the island, was thick enough to ride across.

On the far bank of that great grey highway and downstream a piece was the town of Hannibal, and though it was far, still it was near enough for sound to carry in those stills between gusts of breeze.

With Billy Hawk leading we urged our careful mounts out onto the ice and walked them to the island. The horses stepped easy on the ice, noses down, not trusting it, but they went. We left them there on the island and walked out on the ice again, angling south, feeling the crust below us with each step. A hundred yards out the surface began to feel springy, and beyond that it made little crinkling noises when we stepped.

"This is far enough," Billy said, then cupped his hands to his mouth. His voice carried high and clear out across the remaining stretch of ice. "Halloo, the town!"

At first there wasn't any response, but then we saw men over there, coming out toward the bank. When one of them hailed us, his voice came over thin and distant, but clear.

"Halloo, halloo!"

Billy cupped his hands again, "Hayden party coming in! Can we cross?"

"Bad ice," the voice came back. "Bad ice here! Do you want barges?"

"All you have! Can you break across?"

"We can break and we can barge! Is Mason Chapman with you?"

"He's with us," Billy shouted. "He'll be with the train!"

"Then we'll load at the island!"

We edged back away from the bad ice, then walked back to the island to get our mounts. I was nervous about the ice, but over here away from the main channel it was thick and solid.

"Your horse will tell you," Billy said. "If it's bad ice he won't go on it."

"This is why Chapman was pushing to get started," I surmised.

"Sure. A week from now, maybe two, that ice will be breaking up out there. You ever see a raft in pack ice?"

I hadn't, but I could imagine it. Those big slabs of ice would ride the river and heaven help anything crossing against them.

Even as we climbed the east bank we could hear voices and sounds out there across the river where they were getting crews ready to break out a barge channel.

A short way back from the river was one of those nods, this one a foot-deep frozen gully that would be a rivulet of drainage when the land began to thaw. Billy was leading and stepped his horse across it and into the brush beyond. I had paused a moment to adjust the sling on my arm, and spurred to catch up. The Morgan rose into the easy leap across the gap. I felt a vicious tug at the shoulder of my heavy coat and a gunshot sounded to my left, roaring in the still air. Before I could even turn my head to see where the sound came from we were into the brush. I wheeled the Morgan in a rearing full turn, sank heels in his flanks and went busting right back out of that brush, bearing right. Ahead now was a clear stretch of fifty or sixty yards along the rivulet, and out there framed in the surrounding grey brush was a horseman with a smoking rifle in his hand. He saw me as I saw him, and there was surprise and shock on his face. Then he hauled on the reins, sat his mount on its haunches in a pull-about, and bounded it up the low bank and into the shrubs there, hanging low over his saddle, whipping the horse with his rifle barrel. The Morgan stepped out, took the draw in long paces and veered right into the brush where the rider had gone. Ahead I could hear him pounding away, and ducked low to stay behind him.

That Morgan of mine dearly loved to run, but I was slow and clumsy. With one arm all bound up in a sling I could either rein the horse through the brush or draw my pistol, but not both. I took the reins in my teeth and drew the Walker, then lay low and leveled it past the Morgan's head, waiting for a glimpse to shoot at. There was nothing, and then there was no sound ahead. I pulled up and sat, listening. Nothing stirred. In a minute Billy Hawk came up from behind, rifle in his hand, and then we set out to comb the area. It was only a couple of minutes before Billy found a trail, but about that time we heard hoofbeats, a sudden drumming a ways off, going away. We came together in the brush and looked that way, and Billy shook his head.

"That's a foxy one, Jeremy. We won't catch him now. Are you hurt?"

That was an interesting question, and for a moment there I didn't know. I hadn't thought about it. But I wasn't. There was a hole in the shoulder of my heavy coat and a jagged tear along the back, between the shoulders, where it had billowed out when we jumped the draw.

"I saw him, Billy. It was Walt Murray."

He grinned. "Well, fancy that."

On the way back to the wagon camp one thing was very clear to me. Ready or not, it was time to take my left wing out of storage.

The sun was low and peeking out from beneath the clouds in the west when we pulled in. A lot of the men were out by the trail, most of them armed, and when we came in there were questions of, "What happened? What's the shooting about?" and such. Mason Chapman was there with Hazen Burnett at his side, and Mark Hayden was standing close by with Luther Fritch, burly and heavy-jowled, alongside him.

Chapman said, "What happened out there?"

I pulled rein before him. "Nothing much, except I got shot at by a varmint in the brush."

"Are you all right?"

"Of course I'm all right. It was only Walt Murray. The fellow that hired him," I said, turning to gaze squarely into Mark Hayden's eyes, "made a very poor choice of assassins."

Hayden looked startled, but only for an instant. His immaculate calm was back before you could blink an eye. But the beefy one with him, Luther Fritch, wasn't quite that cool. He looked plainly agitated.

We climbed down and Billy Hawk took our horses. I walked along with Mason Chapman toward his wagon, far enough to fill him in on the incident back there, and some of the others tagged along to listen. Then Billy took over, giving him a report on the river reconnoiter and the barge channel in progress. They walked on and I stopped to let the crowd stream past before going to look for some coffee. When I turned Jenny Sutton was standing there, her eyes big as dollars, her face white. She had been looking at the hole in my coat.

That brought to mind that I had a score to settle with her, and I turned, raised an authoritative finger, and was getting my tongue all set for a lecture, when Mrs. Morton bustled in between us.

"If you lay a hand on that girl I'll have you whipped!" she declared. "You . . . you brute!"

I tried to step around her and another woman was there, Mrs. O'Hannon it was.

"You heard her," she said. "Now you go about your business and let that poor girl alone. You've done more than enough by her already."

Three or four more women were moving in, and Jenny was backing off, wearing a look of pure terror on her face that didn't any more fit Jenny Sutton than galluses fit a goose.

"Ladies," I said politely, "get out of my way. Jenny, damn your hide, you come back here and face the music."

Mrs. O'Hannon stamped her foot, put her hands on her hips and yelled, "Jed!" Next thing I knew there were three or four interested gentlemen around me with scatterguns and muskets aimed at my middle. Mrs. O'Hannon and some of the other women were talking a blue streak, and Mrs. Morton was ushering Jenny away, comforting the poor, dear little thing over the fright she had had.

When they were gone, and at first ebb in the chatter, Jed O'Hannon said, "Now hush up, Grace, everything's took care of. You ladies best go about your business now."

With protests, the women were herded away and the men around me watched them leave. Then one of them, a short, wizened soul to my right, said,

"You're Jeremy Burke, ain't you?"

Jed O'Hannon said, "That's who he is, all right. You recollect, Mr. Burke, we met in Springfield when we signed on. Pleased to have you with us."

The short one said, "My name's Abercrombie, Mr. Burke. I sure am pleased to make your acquaintance." He stuck out his hand and I shook with him. "Likewise." Then the one on my left, a skinny man with a mole on his nose and a bushy beard, said, "My name's Jenkins, Roy Jenkins, and this here . . . behind you . . . is Fred Hollister. We're all with this train, and pleased to have a man of your sort ridin' guard."

I turned a full circle, shaking hands with each one in turn while the others kept their guns trained on me.

"You got the women pow'ful upset," Jed O'Hannon said, apologetically, "what with stealin' that pretty little thing away and usin' her the way you did."

Jenkins cut in, "Not that none of us takes hard of it, Mr. Burke. Fact is, I can't say I blame you. But you know how women can get."

Abercrombie was gazing at the gun at my belt. "Is that the one? By heaven it's big as it said in the newspaper that it was, every bit of it. Man!"

Jed said, "So you see how it is. We all surely bear you no ill will, but all of us got to keep peace in the family, near as possible." He looked around. The women had all gone off somewhere. He breathed a sigh and lowered his gun, and the others did likewise.

"Abercrombie's got some coffee on the fire over by his wagon," Jed invited. "He's a bachelor."

There was a meeting later that evening, around a fire in the clearing next to Luther Fritch's wagon.

Hazen and I were there with Chapman, Mark Hayden, Luther Fritch, the Reverend Reazin, and a dozen other men, others joining as they finished their supper.

Artemis Steen pulled at my elbow. "I've remembered something," he told me quietly.

"From your notes?"

"No, but I recall an article in my paper about a wagon party that disappeared, and there is an odd coincidence . . . ah . . . in the nomenclature."

He had my full attention.

"It wasn't in the report, exactly, but in the original copy before editing there was a list of persons recommended for contact for . . . ah . . . feature material, you know. One of the names, I am positive, was Luther Fritch."

"Was he contacted?"

"Ah, no, I believe most of those listed were unavailable for comment, some having been with the party. You may know of it. It was called the Dinsmore party. An odd coincidence, don't you agree?"

I agreed. The meeting was calling itself to order.

First Chapman told them about the arrangements for crossing the river, and then he had me tell them about the back-shooter out in the brush. Except for four of us—Chapman, Billy Hawk, Hazen, and me—no one else had been let in on the particulars of our hypothesis about how there was a plot afoot against this wagon train and the instigator might be right here with us, so I didn't elaborate. I just told them what had happened.

Then Mark Hayden spoke up in a voice smooth as steeped tea.

"Earlier, Mr. Burke, you named the man who shot at you."

"That's right," I said. "His name is Walt Murray. I've met him before."

"That is very interesting, Mr. Burke. That you would know the man, I mean." He smiled an ingratiating smile. "Don't I recall something about some people following you to Springfield and trying to kill you there?"

"That's right, but they had no connection with Walt Murray." I was beginning to get the drift now.

"I won't dispute your word, Mr. Burke." He smiled again. "But it does seem you get shot at quite a lot."

Chapman was smelling snakes. "He said there was no connection," he pointed out. "What happened today is what we need to concern ourselves with, not this man's private history."

Hayden raised a pleading hand. "No such thing is intended," he said. "I'm just concerned for our party and its safety. It seems to me there is a great deal of coincidence involved here."

Luther Fritch had been sitting there on a folding stool next to Hayden, looking nervous and twiddling his thumbs. Now he spoke up. "Seems funny to me, considering what we have all read about this man in the newspapers, that he would let a man shoot at him, at close range, then let him get away. Seems to me there is something funny going on."

Chapman was looking at them, one and then the other. "What is this all about? Do you have something to say about a man of mine?"

Hayden smiled and looked at Fritch. Fritch looked nervous, but he spoke up right on cue. "We feel," he said, "that Mr. Burke's being with this train jeopardizes the safety of all of us. We have nothing against Mr. Burke, but we feel we would be safer without him here."

The Reverend Reazin, off to my right, stood and turned those marble eyes of his on us, one right after another. "We would go further than that, Mr. Chapman. We are peaceable people, and would go our way in peace. The presence of armed men here," he said, pointing an imperious finger first at me and then at Hazen Burnett, "is just inviting trouble."

Hazen stiffened and started to turn red, but we both held our tongues. This was Mason Chapman's train, and his show. I noticed that Billy Hawk had come in from somewhere and was lounging against a wagon wheel just at the edge of the firelight, a grin on his face like he had come early for Sunday dinner and eaten all the pie.

There isn't anything much more ominous-looking than a grinning Indian.

Mason Chapman leaned back against the grub-box he was propped on and scratched his beard. "I take it you all conc . . . conc . . . agree that we should dismiss our gun-guards before entering Missouri. Is that correct?"

Jed O'Hannon and some of the other men were fidgeting, itching to say a few words, but Chapman silenced them with a raised hand.

"That is correct," Fritch said.

"And you, Mr. Hayden?"

"Reluctantly," he said nodding, "I must agree."

"Reverend?"

"Who lives by the sword shall perish by the sword."

"Now listen, Mr. Chapman," Jed O'Hannon said from the sideline, but Chapman hushed him again.

"That's interesting, because we found something this evening that throws a little different light on things. Billy?"

Billy Hawk turned away from the fire and called, "Bring him in, Willard!" And a moment later Walt Murray stumbled into the firelight, hands tied behind him, old Willard prodding him along with his scattergun. He brought him up into the firelight and stood him there, never taking the scattergun off him. Mason Chapman turned to me.

"Who is this man, Mr. Burke?"

"That's the man I know as Walt Murray. He's the one who shot at me today."

Chapman nodded, and said quietly, "Go ahead, Jeremy, tell us everything you know about this man."

So I did. Most of the men of the wagons were there by then, and some of the women, and a gaggle of children back in the shadows, all ears. I recounted how I had encountered Jake and his boys at that place on the prairie, and how Murray had ridden in, thought I was Jake, and offered work taking out the gun-guards of the train. I didn't know quite what Chapman was up to so I stopped at that, but he urged, "Tell us what else he said to you."

"He said it was 'all set up' for something to happen to this train over in Missouri."

Mark Hayden hadn't moved a muscle, and that icy smile was still on his face, but Luther Fritch had gone white around the jowls. Around the perimeter of the firelight the settlers were whispering and mumbling to one another. Chapman was standing now, thumbs jammed into his belt, heavy shoulders hunched forward, dark-bearded face intent.

Luther Fritch came to his feet, his eyes glinting in the firelight. "That's quite a story," he asserted, "but let's keep in mind that it comes from a man of dubious reputation, a known troublemaker and molester, and one who is well known for telling tall stories."

I was thinking seriously about stepping across there and teaching Luther Fritch a little respect, but Chapman wasn't through yet.

"Of course we need corrob . . . corr . . . supporting evidence," he said. "Mr. Hawthorne, what can you add?"

"I can corroborate that this man was where Mr. Burke said he was, when he said he was, and that Mr. Burke did leave him and three others tied up in a shed," Billy said. "I was there."

Fritch spat. "An Indian. Now really, Mr. Chapman—"

From the shadows between wagons another voice interrupted him.

"I can vouch for every word of it," Jenny Sutton said, stepping into the light. "I heard it all."

This caused a considerable stir, but Chapman silenced it with a hand in the air. "Mr. Hawthorne, tell how you came to find this man."

"I was with Mr. Burke when he was shot at today," Billy said. "Later I watched, and when a man of the train slipped off into the brush, in the direction I judged the assailant had gone, I followed him. The man I followed met this man, then returned to the camp. When he had gone I held a gun on this man and brought him in to talk to Mr. Chapman."

"We've held this man for about three hours now," Chapman told the crowd. "Unfortunately, he refuses to talk to us."

"I could cure that," Billy said quietly, and Chapman said, "That's enough, Billy."

Reverend Reazin had sort of faded back into the shadows, and Luther Fritch was easing back that way, too. I brushed my coattail back away from the butt of the Walker and suggested, "Let's all stay here until we finish talking," and he stopped.

Jed O'Hannon had come forward, and he said to Billy, "Out with it, man. Who was it met this'n in the brush?"

Chapman nodded. Billy said, "It was Mr. Fritch."

Luther Fritch carried an ornate pistol in his waistcoat, and his hand was on it before he noticed that there were two repeating handguns pointed at him, mine and Hazen Burnett's.

Chapman said, "Mr. Fritch, do you have anything to say? No? Well, in that case, there is a constable and a court of justice across the river at Hannibal. I will deliver Mr. Fritch and Mr. Murray to them when we have crossed. Do we have anything else to discuss?"

Jed O'Hannon said, "Seems to me we need to elect a new captain for this party."

Mark Hayden did something then that made me reconsider my hypothesis. His face had gone grey, and his eyes looked first shocked, then hard as cold steel. He strode forward, stood squarely in front of Luther Fritch and stared him in the eye. I thought for an instant there that he was going to hit him. But he just stared.

Then in a low, sad voice, the voice of a man betrayed, Hayden said, "I don't want to believe any of this, Luther, I surely don't. But I just don't know what to think. Can you tell me it's a mistake?"

Fritch lowered his head and said nothing.

"If you will tell me this is a mistake, Luther, I'll defend you to the best of my ability. Just tell me."

Still Fritch said nothing. Hayden looked at him for a long moment, then turned away, his shoulders sagging. He looked defeated.

"It is a hard thing," he said to Chapman, "to recognize betrayal. Mr. Fritch has been a friend to me . . . I have considered him so . . . and I will hope that there is some good explanation for all this, some way to clear his name. But at present it seems I have made a very serious mistake. I'm thankful that you and your men have corrected it before it went too far."

"I bow to your better judgement, Mr. Chapman. Do what you think best for the security of this party. I will back you." He looked around at the people of the train, and said, "I am very sorry." Then he walked away.

Hazen, Billy, Willard, and I got Murray and Fritch safely installed in the back of Fritch's wagon, set a man to guard them, and I looked around for Jenny, but she had gone off somewhere.

I did spot Eleanor Puckett, but Hazen Burnett had got there first and they were having a cosy visit that didn't invite interruption.

So I headed back toward Abercrombie's coffee pot, with that bug-eyed Artemis Steen trailing along behind, scribbling in his pad every time we passed light. At Abercrombie's fire I took off my shirt, unwrapped my shoulder, and began working those protesting muscles, all the time listening to Steen interview himself on the subject of the day's happenings.

CHAPTER THIRTEEN

Fritch and Murray were both gone in the morning, and the fellow who had been standing sentry had a knot on his head and a bad disposition. Billy Hawk found the trail of two horses, heading south. There were a dozen places between here and the town of Louisiana, Missouri, where they could cross the river and leave no trace.

Jed O'Hannon was now captain of the traveling party, and Mark Hayden and the Reverend Reazin seemed subdued. Hayden wore an attitude of regret, saying without words that he had made an error in judgement, tying in with Fritch, and was suitably chastened. Mason Chapman came around and asked me if I wanted to reassess my hypothesis—what he actually said was, "You got second thoughts on how this thing shakes out?" And I allowed I might.

I remember one time when I thought I had made a mistake then it turned out I was wrong. But if I had misjudged Mark Hayden I had misjudged him badly, and I was ready to think the whole thing through all over again. If necessary. Maybe I was all wrong and Hayden was all right and the problem was over. Maybe.

We worked until past noon smoothing and clearing to get the big wagons to the river, then led them one by one out across that hundred yards of hard ice to the island. There were men on the river, cutting a channel fifty feet wide in the crust, starting a string of raftlike barges across, poling and hauling them along the open water, fending them off the ice on the downstream side.

It was near two o'clock when the first barge reached the island, and we all pitched in to build a ramp dock from timbers they brought over with them. Then Jed O'Hannon climbed up on his wagon seat, lined up his team, and walked them out across the timbers and onto the barge lashed at their end. It was a sight to behold, that big wagon tipping and creaking, feeling its way forward onto a floating floor on the lapping water of that channel through the ice.

The wagons went over, two at a time, side by side on the rafts, teams in their traces and wheels lashed to the deck. It was near dark when the final barge tied up at the ramp. We loaded Artemis Steen's surrey and the last two supply wagons aboard. Hazen Burnett had gone across with the first load. I went with the last.

Hannibal was a motley little collection of cabins, huts, storefronts, and fine homes lining both sides of a main thoroughfare almost a hundred yards wide, right down to the river. This broad avenue was the path by which herders from the west prairies brought their flocks to the river in spring and fall to load them aboard steam-powered riverboats for the markets at New Orleans.

There was no traffic now, and we set up our wagon camp right there in the road, square in the middle of town. I doubt if there was a soul in the area that didn't come down to see us, to gawk at the wagons, trade gossip and visit. It had been a long winter, and our arrival was the most interesting thing in months, maybe next to the local fellow who had six fingers on each hand and was thereby a celebrity.

They had received the eastern newspapers, though, and the word got around quickly that this was the party that had that notorious paladin of the pistol, Jeremy Burke, traveling with it. And when that story got mixed in with how that same Jeremy Burke had ridden up on a great fire-breathing black charger and stolen a sweet and innocent princess from her father's castle and carried her languishing on his war saddle across a thousand miles of uncharted wilderness, riding roughshod over renegades all the way, and had saved an entire town from bugs, and had taken a sword thrust through the heart while dispatching about fifty hired mercenaries, and lived to tell of it, it was more than those good folk could ignore. By the time we got settled in for the night, I couldn't go searching for the necessary without half the town tagging along, old men, little kids, and a scattering of robust young ladies who saw themselves as candidates for the paladin's next adventure.

Jenny Sutton, who could have resolved a lot of the misunderstanding, cloistered herself in the Morton wagon and didn't help a bit. Hazen Burnett took in the situation with an amused glance and, seeing as how I was busy, went off to keep Eleanor Puckett from being lonely in this strange place. I decided to think about notching Burnett's ears for him, when I got the time.

When I got my belly full I slipped away and pitched my bedroll under one of the supply wagons and went to sleep.

Pa used to say that the noblest strategy of them all, when things got completely out of hand, was to retreat gracefully and let the situation sort itself out its own way. One time down in Texas he and his company found themselves facing a column of Mexican irregulars across a narrow valley, while behind them a big bunch of renegades with hill Indians among them were coming up on their tail. They dug in, waited for dark, then slipped away in the night, leaving their campfires burning. By morning the battle had been fought, the issue resolved, and Pa and his company took control of the valley without ever firing a shot. You might have heard about that. It was called the San Saba Encounter, and it was one of the things Pa was cited for when they presented him the Whitneyville Walker from Colonel Colt.

I wondered how my folks would have taken to the strange reputation their youngest son had developed since leaving home. Ma might have been upset by it, but I believe Pa would have thought it was funny.

From Hannibal we swung south a few miles to the Spalding licks to take on salt, then headed due west across the high-grass prairie where farmsteads were scattered here and there. For three days out of Hannibal we were still seeing occasional farms, but from there on it was wild and getting wilder.

By the fifth day out we had left all trace of civilization behind. Billy Hawk said there was a little settlement about thirty miles north of us, but it was too far away to look in on. That was the day spring hit. There was a pleasant southwest breeze, high clouds lazing across a high, blue sky, and the morning sun was warm on our backs. Most of the soreness was gone from my shoulder, and I took off my coat, tied it behind my saddle, and let that good sunshine soak into my pores. Billy Hawk had gone on ahead to see the trail, and Hazen and I took turns that day riding out on forward guard. Moving across the wide, tree-dotted prairie it was as though we had the world all to ourselves and it was a good world to own.

Where we were now there was a forested ridge far off to the left, angling in toward our path, and I imagined I could see a trace of new green in the grey of those distant boughs. I was musing on that when I saw a flash of light over there, just an instant flicker like a reflection on glass, nothing more. But it was so out of place, so startling in all that innocent emptiness that it startled me. I was riding about mid-train, and was near Mark Hayden's wagon, and looked around in time to see him turn his head quickly away from the direction I had been looking. There was something so furtive, so secretive in the expression he wore right then that it made my hackles rise. The Reverend Reazin was up with him, and now they had their heads together in private conversations.

We hadn't heard much out of either Hayden or the Reverend since the episode on the river. Hayden was still abashed and apologetic, and the Reverend never had been one to say much except on Sundays.

Two days west of Hannibal had been a Sunday, and he had preached a sermon at sunup before the wagons rolled. Everyone had gathered around and listened politely, and we all prayed together, but there wasn't much handshaking and discussion after. The Reverend Reazin was under the same cloud of doubt that shadowed Mark Hayden, having been thick with Luther Fritch. Up to that point, he had about talked most of the party into pooling their wealth into a common treasury "for protection" and naming him, as a man of God, as purser. Now that was a long way from happening.

All of these people had made a deal with Mark Hayden to buy land in Kansas, and all were carrying the funds to pay him when they arrived there, which meant there was a lot of money stashed away among these wagons.

I kept having a funny feeling about Hayden, but there wasn't anything I could put it to. Mark Hayden had promised these people wagons, supplies, and a trail crew at Springfield, and he had delivered. He had promised them patented land in Kansas, and would be paid for that when he delivered. There was no discernible reason for him to be plotting anything. Sure, there was money here, but he would have a large part of it as soon as we got where we were going, as payment for his land.

Billy Hawk came in that afternoon and we made early camp at the edge of a hardwood grove near the crest of a long swell of ground, almost under that long ridge that we had been closing on all day. When the wagons were placed, the stock tended and the cookfires started, some of us walked to the top of the rise ahead to look around and confer.

"One more day of easy travel," Billy said, "and from there on there's rough land for sixty miles or more. It's rolling, mostly wooded, and some places we'll want anchor lines to hold on the slopes. After that comes the Grand River bottoms, which is very rough country. After that the terrain eases some, up toward St. Joseph."

He and Mason Chapman knew the route, but the rest of us didn't.

Jed O'Hannon was gazing thoughtfully out across those dimming miles. Now he said, "I'm still thinking about what those men said to Jeremy, back in Illinois, about something set to happen over here. The trail ahead, would that be the place, do you think?"

Chapman nodded. "It might be. There is no more isolated place on this road than what we'll travel in the next week or so. I've thought the same thing, Jed. If ever we're vulnerable this side of Westport, it's between here and the Grand. It's close country, with a lot of hills, thick timber in places . . . if I were going to stop a wagon train, that's where I would do it."

"Any particular place?"

"No, just out there somewhere. There are lots of good places for a holdup . . . and I know of nothing else Murray could have been talking about."

"Is there anything we can do about it?"

"Not much. Just keep our guns loaded and our eyes open, and trust to our scout and our guards to see trouble before it happens."

"We'll extend our scouting range," Hazen suggested. "Like we're doing now—one with the train and one looking—but farther out."

I was thinking of one of Pa's stories, the one about King Leonidas and the Spartans. "How about a phalanx," I suggested, and they all looked at me.

"What I mean is, a formation with a defense perimeter, maybe a column of threes or fours. Look, when the train is stretched out and rolling, one wagon after another, the line is nearly a half-mile long. Even closed up, it's too long for two men to protect where visibility is poor. And the men driving are busy driving, they can't watch every stump and draw and still keep their teams on track. With any kind of a force against us, we could be split up and picked off."

"There are places we can't take three or four wagons abreast," Billy said. "All we can do is to pass one at a time."

"Then we'll funnel through those places and reform. Keep a tight formation whenever we can."

"Four rows," Hazen said. "Put the women and supplies in the middle, get all the guns we can on the outside rows. Close 'em up tight, a dozen to a row."

Chapman nodded. "It'll slow us a bit, but we can try it. Starting tomorrow, we travel in phal . . . phal . . . columns of four."

Burnett grinned. "I concur with your hypothesis," he said.

I didn't say anything about the flash on the hill. I'd look into that myself, first thing in the morning.

In the dark before dawn I told Mason Chapman I wanted to look at the ridge top, saddled up the Morgan, and eased him into the hardwood grove alongside our camp, then waited quietly there while below me in the open the wagon camp began to come awake. As soon as there was light to see, I headed out at an angle up the slope, staying to the trees and letting the horse pick his way. The Morgan and I had hunted together a lot back in the hills above Sugar Creek, and he knew we were hunting now. We passed through that dim forest with hardly a sound, climbing as we went, and I reined in at a clear fringe just below the crest.

Time passed, and down below I could hear the mingled sounds of the wagon train getting itself into travel order for the day, then the calls, cracks, and creaks of heavy wagons starting to roll. I waited.

From where I sat the Morgan, blending into the screen of brush at clearing's edge, I could see a good way along the top of the ridge. Eventually the sounds of the train dimmed, moving off along the swell below me, and it was tempting to move around and see how the phalanx was working, but I didn't move. I could tell by the sound when the last wagon rolled over the top of the climb and disappeared down the other side.

Minutes later I found what I was looking for. Up the ridge several hundred yards from where I sat, a covey of pigeons erupted from the treetops and lined out in flight across the crest. There was no good reason why those pigeons would all have flown at once. Without further hesitation I kneed the Morgan up and over the crest of the ridge and partway down the other side, then turned hard right and paced him along the fringe of brush there, angling toward the place where I had seen the birds take flight.

I found their horses in a hollow below the crest where they had made cold camp. There were four horses, three saddles, and one pack frame. Three men, then. They had gone afoot over the crest. I left the Morgan tied in a thicket nearby and went after them. The ridge here was wooded on top, the forest ending abruptly partway down the north side.

I found two of them almost immediately, just inside the edge of the woods, hunkered down with their backs to me, watching intently. Far off on the receding prairie a tight little formation of tall wagons was creeping along, an extended rectangle of migration that from here looked like precision marching order.

If the two watching from the edge of the woods were mystified, I couldn't blame them. That was no way for a wagon train to bunch. Moving from one tree to the next, keeping low, I worked down close behind them. One was Luther Fritch. I didn't know the other, but he was a tough-looking customer. I was hoping to eavesdrop.

I was just easing down behind a screen of brush when I heard a rock torn under a boot behind me and there was no more time for stealth. The third man, the one I knew was there but hadn't seen, had seen me first. If I hadn't heard him he'd have taken my head off with the short spade he carried. He put everything he had into the swing, and as I dropped the sharp edge of that heavy blade scythed through the brush above me. I didn't give him a chance to swing it again. I had turned as I dropped, and I had my feet under me. Every muscle I had went into it as I came out of that crouch, from my legs propelling to my body uncoiling to my right fist coming up from the ground, and I took him square in the face with all of it, just as his spade finished its arc. I could feel things breaking in his face, and the blow lifted him right off the ground. He lit full-out, flat on his back, and the sodden weight of him hitting the ground said he wouldn't move again.

I had come up from the brush like I was trying to fly, and pure momentum carried me right on past him even as he was falling. I felt a twitch at my arm and heard the report of a heavy gun going off, and the sound of a bullet crackling off through the brush. I bounced off a tree trunk, turned half around and got my balance, and saw the tough-looking man who had been with Fritch thumbing back the hammer of a revolving-cylinder rifle for another shot.

The advantage of a rifle over a pistol for close work is that the rifle is carried in hand. The disadvantage is that the man with the rifle thinks he has an advantage. He doesn't know how fast a pistol can be drawn and fired. The rifleman had me cold, and he knew it, and he was much slower in taking his advantage. I didn't waste that time. While he was thumbing his hammer I brought up the Walker and shot him through the lacing on his shirt. There was no time to place the shot. I just took him dead center, and he folded like a rag doll there on the hillside.

I couldn't see Luther Fritch, but I heard a scampering in the brush to my right and headed that way, and stumbled over the man with the spade. That was plain dumb, of course, but I had simply forgotten he was there, and in open woods an inert human body is an obstruction you don't expect to find under your feet. I stumbled and fell, and by the time I got up the sounds of Fritch's retreat were fading. For a big man, he certainly could move.

He would get to the horses if he could, so I ran for the top of the ridge, over the top and down the other side. I was just that much too late. As I got in sight of the horses he was swinging himself into one of them, and it was already digging dirt. I had about one second of view of his back, going away, before he disappeared into the woods below, and I was close enough I could have taken him off that horse. I even had the Walker brought to bear on his broad back. But in my head I could hear Pa saying, "When you must use a gun, boy, always be sure you're in charge of the gun and not the other way around."

I could have killed Luther Fritch right then, but I didn't have to, and if I had touched off that Walker then it would have been in charge of me. I eased the hammer down and put the gun away, and he was gone.

I wouldn't catch him now, not in those thickening woods to the west. I went back and got the Morgan, then gathered up their three remaining horses and equipment, and went back over the top of the ridge. The wagon party was still in sight out there on the rolling plain, but it had stopped moving and there were horsemen making time back toward me. They had heard the shooting.

I didn't know either of the men on the ground. They were both rough-hewn, bearded men, both in woodsman's clothing, and both were dead. I felt cold and distressed looking down at the one with the hole through him. I had shot and killed another man, and I guessed I never would get used to that. But I felt even worse when I looked at the other one. There is something removed, something impersonal, about killing with a gun. There is nothing impersonal in breaking a man's head with your fist. Both of them had died instantly. I noticed I had another hole in my coat, this one a rip along the arm that had taken out half the lower seam. It was beginning to look doubtful that this coat would last out the season.

It was a chore loading them onto their horses. Both were big men, and the one who'd had the spade was at least as big as me. I worked up a sweat getting them draped over their saddles and lashed in place.

Hazen Burnett and five of the settlers met me coming down off the ridge.

CHAPTER FOURTEEN

We took the time to bury those two bushwhackers on a rise in the prairie, where the ground was beginning to thaw, and after I filled Mason Chapman in on what had happened he called the party together so they could all hear it. Two of the horses I brought in were the ones Fritch and Murray had taken when they escaped. Nobody knew the two dead men.

The incident brought home to all of them that we had a problem, and it was Mason Chapman who put the proportions to it.

"In this party there are forty-four overland wagons," he explained. "They are worth eighteen hundred dollars apiece in St. Louis. Each of you is carrying the money you'll need to buy the land you've contracted for in Kansas, and some more to get established and get a crop in the ground. That is maybe three thousand dollars per wagon on the average, and I'd guess more in some cases. Then there is the stock. Oxen broken to the trace are bringing upwards of a hundred dollars in St. Louis right now, saddle stock is worth more than that, and a milk cow sells for fifty if it isn't dry. Then there are your supplies, your tackle, your furnishings, tools, implements, guns, and valuables.

"Look around you. Any settlement train is a rolling treasury, and this one is double rich because you haven't patented your lands. What law exists in

Missouri right now is only around the edges, and the edge we're heading for has a full-scale war going on. Bushwhackers, Free-Staters, and the so-called Jayhawkers right in the middle of it.

"And we, by virt . . . virt . . . because of being immigrants from the northern states, are Jayhawkers. You all knew that when you signed up for this passage. What you didn't know . . . what none of us knew until now . . . was that somebody has singled this train out for special attention. Based on what we know now, we must assume that there is an organized force that intends to attack and rob this party."

Abercrombie had his face scrunched up in that scowl he always got when he tried to think about things he hadn't thought about much before. He asked, "What were those fellers doin' up there when you come on 'em, Jeremy?"

"Best I could tell, they were just keeping an eye on this train. Yesterday they were trying to signal somebody down here."

"You saw them yesterday, too?"

"Late yesterday. That's why I went up there this morning, to take a look."

"But who would they be signalin' here?"

There wasn't any answer to that. They just all looked around at each other.

"We'd best get rolling," Chapman said, finally. "We've lost three hours today, but there's still time to make another five or six miles by dark."

"We gonna keep to this columns-of-four stuff?" Hollister asked. "It's hard drivin' that way."

"I think you should," I told Chapman. "I saw the train from up top awhile ago, and I sure wouldn't want to rush up on the flanks of that formation."

"We'll stay with it for a while," Chapman said.

"It hasn't slowed us any."

"I'd sure like to know if somebody here is in with them outlaws," Hollister said.

"We'll meet tonight and talk some more. Now let's get to rollin'."

We added another four miles that day to the one the train had made during the morning, and it was a tired, cranky, and worried bunch that gathered among the clustered wagons after dark.

Billy Hawk had been far out ahead, and Hazen and I had scouted a mile out on each side, and none of us had seen anything amiss. But it had been a chance to do some hard thinking.

Mark Hayden wasn't the only man on this trip whose past was sketchy. I could pretty well eliminate most of the emigrants. They had wives and kids with them, and I couldn't see a man planning massacre putting his family in the middle of it. I knew enough about Chapman and Burnett that I didn't have any serious doubts about them. But there were some odd members. Abercrombie didn't have any family with him, for one. And that nutty journalist, Steen. No, I just couldn't see it.

The one with most opportunity to betray the train was the scout, of course. He came and went. But Billy Hawk had been the one who stirred the pot in the first place, and why would he do that if he was in it?

It came back to Hayden, but that now seemed very unlikely. What could he have to gain?

But if it wasn't Hayden . . . I had a feeling I'd missed a step someplace. For some reason I kept remembering a thing Pa had said: "Men never fight over land. What they fight over is possession. Land is something you live on and use. Possession is something you put down on paper."

An odd thought. But it kept coming back, and I kept chewing on it. I felt like Pa could have given me the answer. For my part, though, I couldn't even get the question straight.

It was due to be an angry meeting that night, and it was. Everybody there was fixing to point the finger at everybody else. Mason Chapman looked worried and serious. "We've got to get to the bottom of this thing," he told them, then turned to face Mark Hayden. "Mr. Hayden, I think you'd better tell us all about your association with Luther Fritch."

It was in how he said it, I suppose, but Hayden got indignant. "Now see here, Chapman! If you have any accusation to make, you'd better prove it."

Abercrombie said, "I don't recollect any accusations."

Jed O'Hannon eyed Hayden narrowly. "Does the shoe fit, mister?"

Hayden looked around him and paled. He had handled that wrong, and he knew it. It was no time for indignation, but he couldn't back up now. All those welling suspicions were right back on his shoulders again.

If Hayden were guilty, he had just made a bad error. He had underestimated a lot of people. Proof and substantiations are for courts. People in the real world observe, and infer, and make judgements every day of their lives, and those judgements are more critical than the judgements of courts because they have to be.

Assuming Hayden was our culprit, he had just overdrawn and now he had to play his hand.

"I resent being singled out like this," he told Chapman. "Because of my unfortunate association with Mr. Fritch, you make me feel convicted. Convicted of what? I ask one of you to name one thing I am guilty of. Is there one agreement I have made that I did not keep? You paid for wagons and supplies, you have wagons and supplies."

"That's true," a man said.

"You were to form in Springfield to go west with a wagon master and crew. I have arranged all that!"

Fred Hollister nodded. "You did that, right enough." Several others nodded reluctant agreement.

"I hired you the best wagon master available," Hayden said, shifting an accusing gaze at Chapman, "though it seems now he lacks loyalty to the man who hired him."

Chapman scowled. "My commitment is to no man, Mr. Hayden. I signed to take a wagon party to the Neosho Valley, Kansas Territory, and to guide and safeguard that party and its members. From the day we left Springfield, my obligation has been to this train, not to the agent who solic . . . sol . . . hired me. Let's have that clear."

"Be that as it may," Hayden said and turned from him to where Jed O'Hannon and several other stood, concerned and intent. "You people made a contract with me, and I have kept my part to the letter. Now, am I being accused of something? Or what? Some wild supposition dreamed up by an Indian? Some string of chance incidents related by the imaginations of a bunch of ruffians?"

Hayden had their rapt attention. He had a golden tongue, all right. He was innocent and righteously indignant. A little off-stride, maybe, but I could surely see the possibility of our suspicions of him being in error. What, in fact, would he have to gain?

Again, I thought of that remark my pa had made about land and possession and paper. It kept coming back.

Hayden wasn't through. He still had his best shot to fire.

"Assume for the moment," he pleaded, an insulted angel defending his shining honor, "that I did have some mysterious plot to steal from you in some way. You have paid me for your conveyance and travel. I already have received that from you. Most of the rest of what I assume you carry would be payment for your land, and when you receive your lands, I will have that. What possible reason could I have for stealing it from you in advance?"

And there it was. What Pa had said and what Hayden said all came together and came out clear. I knew what the game was.

Hayden put his hands on his hips and stood tall, letting that sink in. There was silence. These were mostly good, honest people, and they weren't practiced at thinking in devious ways. What he said, on the surface, took them cold, without a ready answer.

I decided the wavering silence had gone on long enough. There was a good chance they would decide he was right and Chapman was wrong. It wouldn't be the first time a golden tongue had swayed good people from what their common sense told them was right. How else does a politician ever get elected to office?

"You'd have a point there, Mr. Hayden," I said quietly, "if there was land for these folks to go to."

I was playing a hunch, but as soon as I said it I knew it was right, and so did the others. Hayden turned white as a ghost.

Jed O'Hannon looked stunned. "No land? No land in Kansas? My Lord!"

"I suggest that there is no land for you in the Neosho Valley, or anywhere else, at least not that Mr. Hayden can deliver. I suggest that the entire purpose of assembling this party was just what Billy said: to put a rolling treasury in the Missouri badlands where it could be taken without too much trouble."

O'Hannon held up a hand. "Now just a minute, Jeremy. There is a patent on that land. We all saw it."

"I'm sure you did. And what happens to a land patent when the land is sold off? Does the buyer get the patent papers to keep?"

"We'll have deeds," O'Hannon pursued, "deeds based on the patent."

"But Mr. Hayden would keep the patent instrument itself. How many times, Mr. O'Hannon, do you suppose a patent could be sold as long as nobody shows up to demand a deed?"

Somebody breathed, "My God!"

An older man in the fringes of the crowd said, "But I sold everything I had to come out here. All I got now's what's in my wagon. There has to be land!"

Grace O'Hannon spoke from over to one side, where some of the women had gathered to listen. "Is that right, Jed? What he says?"

O'Hannon was silent for a moment. Then he nodded, a haunted look in his eyes. "It's right."

Billy Hawk had moved up beside me. He whispered, "You've hit it. That's what's going on."

Hayden's voice was shaking. "Listen, all of you. You have my word there is land for you. I told you there is!"

177

Old Mr. Puckett quavered, "I got nowhere else to go, Mr. Burke. I got everything I own staked on this move. There has to be land out there. There just has to be."

Follis Holt was shaking his bearded head slowly, like a bear in torment. "My kids are gonna grow up on new ground. We can't go back. There ain't anything to go back to."

"There's land," a determined voice said from the ranks. "Fourteen years I been puttin' back for a new start, and I ain't gonna give it up now. I say there's land out there waitin' for us!"

Someone else said, "But he may be right. How do we know?"

Asa Miles turned a hard stare on Chapman. "If you knowed all this, how come it didn't come out 'til now? Why didn't we know this back in Springfield? Why wait 'til now?"

Chapman held up an imperious hand. "All right, that's a good question, Mr. Miles. First, we didn't know it. Billy thought there was something haywire about this setup, but we couldn't put a finger on it. Billy tracked over half the country trying to learn something, but we didn't know. We just suspected. It wasn't until we got Fritch paired up with that outlaw, Murray, back at the river, that we even knew for sure something was wrong. And it wasn't until now, thanks to Mr. Burke here, that we had any idea what it might be. We've been going on hypoth . . . hypoth . . . hunch, Mr. Miles. And to some extent we still are."

"That's right, we don't know!" Mr. Miles said. "What's to say this whole crazy idea isn't just what Mr. Hayden said it was, a pipe dream!"

"There are two dead men back there," I pointed out, "that says it's no pipe dream."

"Second," Chapman continued, "suppose we had learned all this, say, at Hannibal. What would you have done? Gone back east? Gone to St. Louis or up to the Great Lakes? Sat right where you were? My guess is you'd have gone as many directions as there are wagons in the party, and mostly wound up nowhere, if you'd known this for a fact, back there. I'm hired to run and safeguard a wagon train, Mr. Miles, and I can't do that if it scatters to the four winds. Where we are now, there is no law but us, and no protection except ourselves. We'll go where the party decides to go, but by Heaven we'll all go together!"

"I tell you," Hayden shouted, "there is land. Plenty of land, rich, black ground waiting to be broken. Trust me!"

"Trust him, hell," someone said, "let's hang him."

Jed O'Hannon turned on them. "Now hold on! There'll be no such talk as that. It strikes me what Mr. Chapman and Mr. Burke say might be true. But we don't know that for absolute sure, now do we? We can't know that until we get to Kansas. In the meantime, we got some decidin' to do. Mr. Chapman's right. Wherever we go, we better be together in it."

The talk went from there, and I could see it was going to be a long evening. Mark Hayden just sort of slunk away, finally, back to his wagon at the edge of the gather. The Reverend followed him.

I asked Chapman, "Have you been paid yet?" He looked at me a long moment and then motioned Hazen and me to come along and headed for the Hayden wagon. With us to back him, he got paid on the spot for the whole trip, the whole contract. I was interested in that, because if he didn't get paid he couldn't very well pay me my hundred dollars guard money when we got wherever we were going.

The settlers finally took a tentative vote that night, and they voted to go on to Kansas. It was two things: abiding faith that somehow all this was wrong and there would be farmsteads waiting for them when they got there, and the fact that most of them didn't have anyplace better to go.

When morning came and Hayden and the Reverend were gone, the faith part wore pretty thin, but still they decided to go on.

Those two had skipped out during the night, riding the horses Hayden kept separate at his wagon and carrying whatever they could carry on horseback. Their wagons were just left standing where they were. Their trail led west, and a few miles out it angled south, and then we lost it.

"One thing sure," Hazen said, "they sure aren't aiming for where we came from."

Billy Hawk turned a deadpan, Indian face on him. "I concur," he said, "with your hypothesis."

"One thing is bothering me about what Hayden's trying to do," Hazen said, "and that is, it looks to me it would take quite an organization to set up an ambush of a train this size, and that means money from someplace. Has Hayden got that kind of money to hire men and such? And if he's got it, where did he get it?"

"He sold the wagons," Billy suggested.

"But he had to pay for them so he could sell them. There isn't much money in that."

"Nor in supplies, either. And he has laid out a lot of money in arrangements for this party. So where did he get it all?"

"Probably from the people he sold the Kansas land to the first time," I said. "I'd bet that land is being farmed right now by folks with valid deeds to it. Billy, you've been there. What's there?"

"When I was in Kansas was four years ago. There was hardly even a Kansas then. And I never saw the Neosho Valley. I just know where it is."

"I wish we knew what Hayden will do now," Hazen said.

Billy took off his top hat, wiped his brow on a coat sleeve and reset the hat squarely on his head. "He'll do exactly what he set out to do. He hasn't any choice, that I can see. He has to take this train."

"What I wish I knew," I told them, "is how he'll go about it now that he knows we know he's coming."

By the end of that day we were out of prairie and into country more wooded than not, hardwood groves spreading before and closing behind us, miles on end of woodlands where the hills got steeper and the valleys got deeper, and those wagon folk were getting a good taste of the hard work of moving overland caravans through wilderness. When the going was hard, they all pitched in to help each other. They hadn't done that before, back in the Mississippi bottoms. Out here in the "lost lonesomes," as Asa Miles called it, our motley group was becoming a community.

The train held stubbornly to its phalanx order, although it slowed things down a bit, and there were always guards at night. Pausing on a hillock in late afternoon to watch the close columns of bright canvas creep by below, I tried to think it out. If I were a marauder, and bent on reducing that force, how would I go about it? I had to admit, it wouldn't be easy. An attack from the front would be disastrous. Chapman had drilled the men enough to know what to do, and it was obvious to anybody watching that pack of wagons that it would be a moment's work to swing out, open the front rows and present a deadly barrage of rifle fire.

Neither would I attack broadside, at least not without good cover to charge from or to snipe from. The rear would be most vulnerable to damage, but that was where the least damage could be done in an open attack.

And all of that, in all cases, assumed the attackers could get past Hazen and me. That wouldn't be easy. I knew what I could do if pressed, and I was pretty sure Hazen Burnett, in his own way, could be just as deadly.

Thinking on it while the Morgan stood at rest beneath me, I drew the Walker to check its loads. The beeswax seals were tight on the cylinder bores, and the wax around the caps was intact. That meant a reliable load, wet or dry, day after day, and no misfires. The big gun gleamed in my hand in the late sunlight, dark-bright metal and burnished wood, big and businesslike and utterly lethal. It was the nearest thing to a handcannon in the world.

As the wagons crept on by toward their night camp at a spot Billy had selected a mile on, I watched the warming sun drop huge and red across the grey-feathered hilltops, striking amber into the branches and shooting rays of gold through the few strung-out clouds above it, and thought again of Asa's expression, "the lost lonesomes." Well, I realized I wasn't lost out here, not even a little bit. In a way that was surprising to realize; I felt like I was right at home. I was king of the hill in the midst of a splendor so vast the eye got lost in the distance. I wasn't lost. That beckoning sun seeking its horizon pointed the way toward home, not away from it.

Out there . . . that was what it was. Out there. How can a man be lost when he is right where he belongs?

Pa always said the problem with waxing poetic is you can't do that and pay attention at the same time. He used to tell about a fellow that got caught with his fantasies hanging out. He was a scout for Captain Clark in the Shawnee troubles, and he was checking trail when he stepped out in the middle of a spring glade that struck him so pretty he got all gullet-bound and commenced to spouting verse right there in heathen territory. Upshot of it was a Shawnee raiding party walked right up on him while he was absorbed in imagery. They cut off his lyrics and planted a tomahawk in his second stanza.

Pa was right. I was so near to drowning in that lonesome sunset that I didn't hear a thing until something prodded me between the shoulder blades and I said, "Hoop!" and came within a hair of bailing off my horse and opening fire on all and sundry.

"Some gun-guard you are," Jenny Sutton said. "If I'd been a yayhoo I could have laid you low. You didn't even know I was here."

I had shifted half around in the saddle, the wrong direction, and if the Morgan had been of a mind to shy right then it and me would have parted company. Generally I am contained under stress, but for a moment there I plumb lost my aplomb and like to broke my good arm wagging the Walker in her face and hollering, "Jenny, damn your hide, I might have killed you when you did that!"

"You wouldn't do any such thing, Jeremy Burke. Turn around. You're twisted like a pea vine."

I got turned around and put the Walker away, then gave her the fiercest glare I had ever unleashed on anybody. "That has to be the foolest thing you ever did. What are you doing up here, anyway? Why aren't you with the wagons? And pull down that skirt, for Heaven's sake. Your whole bare legs are showing!"

"So who's to see?" She tossed her head. "There isn't anybody up here but us and a lot you care about my bare legs, anyway. I got tired of riding in a wagon. I came to see what you're doing."

"Jenny," I started, and then looked away. The way she sat, astraddle of the dapple pony on Walt Murray's old saddle, her skirt hiked up way beyond decent, I was getting cross-eyed trying to concentrate on her pommel. Damn beautiful sunsets, anyway. I mean, did you ever notice how a woman's thigh sort of curves and glows like amber when there is saddle leather pressing it from inside and the red of sundown hits it full? A man hasn't got any business noticing things like that about a tagalong girl who has never been anything but a nuisance.

I gave up trying to reconstruct my aplomb and handed her my coat. "Put this over your lap. Did anybody else see you riding like that?"

"Of course not. I rode sidesaddle until I was away from the train. Golly, it's pretty up here, isn't it? Here, hold my rifle."

For a small girl, Jenny has long legs, and what with all that skin shining there I hadn't even noticed she was carrying her old rifle. I guess that was what she prodded me with. I held her rifle and looked off at the other scenery while she covered herself with my coat. "Now, what are you doing up here?"

"I got lonesome. Do you know you haven't said boo to me since we crossed the river? You're not angry with me or anything, are you, Jeremy?"

"Oh, no! Angry? Not much! What would I be angry about? Certainly not because everybody in that train down there thinks I am some sort of heathen monster that carries off little girls and dallies them halfway across the country, and then I get guns pointed at me because of it. And certainly not because I've been trying to send you home where you belong since Springfield and you're still here. I ought to paddle your tail is what I ought to do."

"I can be anywhere I want to be, Jeremy Burke. You're not my mother. Besides, all I wanted to do was ask you something."

"Well, what?"

"Well, all that time when we were alone out there, after you spirited me away and carried me off into the—"

"Damn it, Jenny, I didn't do any such thing. Those people just think I did because that's what you told them."

"Watch your language. Anyway, if it had been like that, and we'd been all alone out there all that time like we were, I expect you would have done all sorts of things . . . I mean, had your way with me, and . . . oh . . ."

Her eyes had got bigger and bigger as she talked, and she was blushing worse than the sunset. And I expect I was redder than she was. But I took some deep breaths and hung in there. "So?"

"Well, of course, if you had ever . . . I mean even tried to . . . well, of course I wouldn't have stood for any such goings on, but . . . well . . ."

Now those eyes were full round and warm and wet and there were fires there to consume a man, and I had never seen such fires, but then they changed and her jaw went tight and suddenly she was mad clear through. "Well," she almost shouted, "I just wanted to say you could at least have tried!"

I don't know when I got my mouth closed but it was sometime later, after she had flung my "damned old coat" at me and grabbed her rifle and put heels to the dapple and disappeared into the shadowing woods below.

What she had done to me there just had to be from ignorance. Girls surely don't have any notion of the kind of chaos they can unleash in an unsuspecting man when they go to displaying a lot of well-constructed thigh and catching the sunlight in their eyes and calling up visions of private delicacies on the prairie.

"Two times two makes four," I told the Morgan horse.

Pa always said that a man's will is what sets him above the critters who are victims of their own juices. He said a man is stronger than the carnal lures of nature and can will them away.

"Two times three makes six," I told the horse.

Man is a creature of choice and judgement, Pa always said, and that applied to women as well as to other situations. A man can think clear thoughts and be unswayed by any primal itch in his belly or throbbing in his loins.

"Two times four makes eight," I insisted. "Two times five makes ten."

As man is the master of his fate, Pa said, so is he the master of his own body. The key is concentration.

Ma never said a lot, but one thing she did tell me: don't believe everything your father says.

"Two times six makes twelve. Two times seven . . ." I was into the four timeses before I decided pure will wasn't going to hack it and I had better find myself a creek and take a good, cold bath.

Billy Hawk came into camp late that night on an exhausted horse.

"I found them," he told us. "They've got a regular outlaw's nest at Camden Road Cut. If they don't hit us between here and there we'll have to go right into them. There's no good way around."

CHAPTER FIFTEEN

The following day the wagons didn't move. We had high land and a good field of view, so Mason Chapman circled them there, tongue to tailgate, and mounted heavy guard on wagons and stock while the three of us who were being paid to take damn fool chances rode out on far reconnaissance.

Camden Road Cut, as Billy described it, was due west of us about twelve miles . . . two days' travel for the wagons or a half day for riders. The "cut" was a wide place in a deep gorge where traffic could cross. The gorge was at the beginning of the breaks of the Grand River in rough country and there wasn't anyplace else to cross it unless we swung south into country even worse.

The "outlaw's nest" he described was an encampment right down in the gorge, at the cut. There were a lot of men there. Billy guessed maybe thirty, and a rough bunch.

If we had been hoping—which we had—that what we had to face when the showdown came was a half-dozen casual thieves who would turn tail at a confrontation, the news put an end to that. The hunters were out in force and we were ducks on the pond.

At first light, on fresh horses, Billy Hawk rode north, I rode south, and Hazen Burnett rode east. What we were looking for was reinforcements or an escape route, whichever came first. None of us held much hope of finding a cavalry regiment in the middle of the Missouri wilds, but it wouldn't hurt to look.

We were fifty miles from any known settlement, where we were, and well into the rough lands, so there wasn't likely even a cluster of farms nearby. The road we were on was no road at all, only a passage route that was known and sometimes used in season. But in this season there would be no one on it. Mark Hayden had planned well, putting this rolling treasury in the middle of some of the lonesomest land east of the territories at a time of year when no bystanders might happen along, and in a manner that nobody would be looking for us, either ahead or behind.

But looking was worth a try.

I headed out south by east in a long loop, trying to take in as much terrain as I could in the daylight hours, looking for . . . something . . . anything to help get a bunch of decent people out of a bad bind.

When I left Indiana on that cold night I gave up home and the comfort of kin around me. I didn't regret it. I was born with a westering in my blood and I always knew one day I'd go. But that never made me a loner.

The people in those wagons, with their hopes and dreams and families to care for, they were my people now. They were going my direction in more ways than I had known. I had thought to go a direction. They *had* a direction. I had started out going away from something, and had found people going toward something, and their something had become mine . . . a dream, a chance for a better life, a chance to raise families on clean soil. I found I wanted that, too. Somewhere back there I had set my hopes on having a place to go.

I didn't know where it might be—maybe Kansas, maybe somewhere else—but it was there waiting and all I had to do was find it. Like Jed O'Hannon, or Abercrombie, or Asa Miles, or any of them. They didn't know where it was, either, but when they knew they had been cheated they didn't turn back. Maybe their place wasn't the place they thought, but there was a place for them and they meant to find it.

I meant to find it, too.

And when I did I'd need someone to share it. Because, I realized, that's what it was all about.

The country to the south was rugged land, mostly hills with rough breaks scattered through them and more forest than not. I was up on one of Chapman's saddle stock, a blaze dun with the soul of a hitch-ox. He wasn't much for sudden, but once set on a path it never dawned on him to stop.

We made miles, and though I was searching hard—for sign of civilization, for a way to get help, for a plan of some kind—I found nothing. Just wild country too remote from the main roads to have drawn settlements and too rough, mostly, to have attracted any farmer's plow. I swung south, then a ways east, and sometime after midday I pointed the dun north and started back. I was discouraged, but maybe Hazen or Billy would find something.

I was an hour toward the wagon train when the dun perked its ears and looked east, and I eased us back into brush to see what was coming.

I saw them a while before they saw me. There were two of them, rough men who knew their way in this wild country, and they rode as though they knew where they were going. They followed no path that I could see, but rode as though they had been this way before. Both were heavily armed. They weren't going toward the wagon train. They were aimed for somewhere beyond it.

You know, a fellow can concentrate so hard that after a while his concentrator gets numb and he can walk right up on what he has been looking for all day and hardly know it.

What I had been looking for, in a general sense, was an opportunity. These two yayhoos weren't much of one, but they were better than nothing.

So I let them go by and pulled right in behind them and asked, "You boys heading for the cut?"

I had startled them like that on purpose, because I hoped at least one of them would go for a gun and give me a chance to show off. It's awfully hard to explain to a stranger just how desperate and dangerous you are. It's easier if he lets you show him. They did and I did. Their sidearms weren't even out of the leather yet when I gave them a look at the hellhole in the front of the Walker.

"Don't get hostile," I told them. "I might be your long-lost cousin."

A Walker's muzzle is a powerful pacifier. They both got their hands into plain sight and sat right still.

"Do we know you?" the skinny one said.

"No, but I expect you know about me. I'm a pistol prodigy."

They looked at each other, then the grizzly one cocked an eyebrow. "You're a what?"

"You know," I said, "a knight errant of the revolving handgun. One of those emerging in our troubled land possessed of a formidable skill surpassing even the deadly arts of the fencing master. I am abroad upon the land now in quest of daring-do and tidy fortunes. Hell, you know. It's in all the newspapers."

"It is?" Skinny goggled at me.

Grizzly was quicker on the uptake. "You ain't claimin' to be that there pistol paladin, are you?"

"Well, maybe not the exact same one, but I'm one of 'em. See, I even use a Walker."

"Yeah, I can see that. But I know you ain't that same one. The papers say he always rides a blazing steed, and what you got there is just a blaze dun. It ain't the same."

"Well, I'm working up to that."

"Ain't that the way it always is?" Skinny said sourly. "Fellow gets his name in the paper and right away every yayhoo in the country wants to be just like him."

"Well, what do you want with us?" Grizzly asked.

"I want to know if you're on your way to the cut."

"We might be. How come you want to know?"

"Well, I heard a bunch of the boys are up there, and they need to know there's a bunch of cavalry coming their way."

"Cavalry? You seen 'em?"

"I seen enough of them."

"Well, how big a bunch is there? A patrol, a company? What?"

"Big enough bunch to have a bugler."

They looked at each other again and got right worried.

"That's pretty big," Skinny said.

"Sounds like it," Grizzly allowed. Then to me he asked, "How come you don't come along and tell 'em yourself?"

"I'll be along directly, but I got other things to do first. Will you boys spread the word? I meant that about the bugler, and I wouldn't lie to you. I'm a

Hoosier."

"A what?"

"You can count on it," I assured them, then edged the dun off to the right and lit out east.

I admit that encounter wasn't much to show for a whole day's ride through bad country trying to save a bunch of desperate settlers, but it was the best I could do.

Pa used to say that in any encounter, you have an advantage if you can confuse the enemy. In this situation now, though, it was pretty hard to tell who the enemy was, so I figured I'd just play it safe and confuse everybody.

Hazen Burnett had already come in when I got back to the train that evening, and Billy Hawk came in a little after dark. Their luck hadn't been any better than mine.

Billy had found a camp of Indians up in the hills north of us, but they weren't interested in white people's fights. They had learned a long time ago that whenever Indians get involved in squabbles between whites, the way it gets resolved is the whites quit squabbling and all gang up on the Indians, and they wanted no part of it.

Hazen hadn't seen anybody at all. Couple of times on his way back in he said he had the feeling he was being followed, but he didn't see a soul.

The weather being dry, Mason Chapman had had men out all day hauling wood and digging several banked trenches around the wagon perimeter so that pit fires could be set. He was concerned about a night attack and it turned out he was right. Maybe it was because the train had stopped and was no longer moving west. Whatever the reason, they came at us just past midnight.

It was pitch dark, and a poor time for either attack or defense. It began with a rush on the draft stock, which Chapman had grazing out on the flats. We heard some shots fired out there, and then some more, and before any of us could get organized Mason Chapman came boiling out of his wagon dressed in hat, boots, and longhandles and commenced to giving orders right and left.

"Douse them fires," he shouted. "Put out your lanterns. Train guards to me!"

When we got to him, in the middle of the dark enclave, he was calling out names. "Asa! Brian! Jacob! Farley!" and the selected settlers were answering from here and there.

"Pit fires and cover fire!" Chapman hollered, and in the darkness I heard men moving. It was one of the things he had drilled them for, ever since we passed Hannibal. Now they moved and they knew what to do. There was more gunfire from the direction of the herd, and now there were rifle balls singing around in the wagon enclave.

"Women and children, stay in the wagons!" Mason bawled. Billy! Hazen! Jeremy! Here!"

"I'm here," I said. Hazen answered from a few feet away, "Here!" Billy's voice in the darkness was right beside me, though I hadn't heard him. "Here, Mason."

"Billy, you go for the stock. Bring them in between fourteen and seventeen. Willard is movin' my rig and the supply wagon right now. Go get 'em."

Billy didn't answer, but I knew he was on his way.

"Hazen, get on the south ring. Jeremy, north. If you see somebody that don't belong here, shoot him."

"I can't see a damn thing," Hazen groused.

"Just get yourself a position. You will."

A ball whipped past and thudded into a wagon bed someplace. I heard kids whimpering and women calming them. I headed blind for the north side of the ring, and when I bumped into a wagon I got down and crawled under it. There were men there. As I came in one of them fired into the darkness and somebody a few feet away said, "Hold your fire, damn it. I'm out here."

"Who's out there?" I called, keeping my voice low.

"John Brent. I'm tryin' to light this fire. Don't shoot at me."

"Let him get it lit," I ordered. "He's one of ours."

"I can't see anything," one of them said.

"Well, if you can't see it, don't shoot it."

Then there was a spark, and a glow. Farther out in the flats a gunshot stabbed the darkness and splinters flew from the wagon above us. I lined the Walker on the place the shot had come from. "Brent, is that anybody of ours?"

"No, that must be one of them."

"Then drop down a minute, will you?"

"I'm already down."

I let the Walker go and put a ball where that gunshot had come from and heard somebody yip out there. The big handgun's roar was deafening.

"Sounded like you hit one," the man beside me said.

"I doubt it."

The glow became a light and flared beyond the dirt bank as Brent came crawling back in under the wagon. "Got 'er started," he said. Along the wagon circle other pit fires were coming alive, throwing their fitful light outward from the banked dirt between them and the wagons. There was movement out there, and the firelight caught someone in relief for a moment. I fired again and saw him drop, then other men opened up around me.

There was other firing now, around the circle of wagons, as the pit fires lighted targets here and there. Only at the rear flank did it remain dark, to give Billy and the herdsmen a corridor to bring in the stock.

Somebody else came crawling in under the wagon just as I fired again, and slid right in close beside me, and in the reek of gunsmoke I smelled vanilla. The newcomer let off a round at somebody moving out past the pit fire, then I felt a hand on my shoulder.

"Jeremy? Is that you?"

I already knew who it was. "Jenny, what are you doing here? You're supposed to be in Mrs. Morton's wagon."

"I didn't know where you were until I heard that pistol of yours shooting. How many of them are there out there?"

"I haven't the vaguest idea. Keep your head down."

"Are we going to die here, Jeremy?"

"I think that's what those people out there have in mind. Whoop!" I saw one and let off a shot just as somebody else fired, and the man out in the firelight flopped backward.

"I got him," somebody said.

Jenny had snuggled in so close to me I didn't even have room to squirm. "Jeremy, back there when you tried to send me home, the reason I didn't go was I wanted to stay with you."

"Well, now you see what it's got you."

"Well, I don't care. If you just weren't so arbitrary about . . . just a second." She rolled hard against me and let off another shot with her brother's old repeating rifle. Then she turned again and she was nestled under my arm, her breath warm on my face. I found I was having a hard time concentrating on the job at hand.

"Jenny, damn it, you're deviling me!" I whispered.

"Mind your language. If we're about to die here, I want to know . . . you do want me, don't you, Jeremy?"

A ball from the darkness ricocheted off an iron hub and threw gravel in front of us. Another splintered wood somewhere above. There was no return fire from our wagon. Jenny's breath, right there at my lips, smelled sweet and warm. The other breaths, one at each ear and one tickling the hair on my neck, smelled like onions and tobacco.

"Well?" one of them said.

When I turned my shoulder bumped a man on one side and my elbow got another one. "What the hell are you fellows doing? We're supposed to be standing off outlaws here!"

"Yeah, right," one of them allowed. "But how about it? Do you want her or not?"

"Get to firing!" I shouted, and they slithered over and went to work.

"Well?" Jenny asked.

It was more than I could handle. "Well, yeah, of course I do, Jenny, and you just devil the pants off me. But I haven't got time to—"

"Ah," Jenny sighed contentedly. "I knew you did. Kiss me, Jeremy."

A ball whined past so close it cut my hat brim and I leveled the Walker and put two shots right back down the path of it. In the darkness off to the right there was the muted thunder of moving animals.

Billy was bringing in the herd. Sustained covering fire erupted from that end of the enclave and I could hear Mason Chapman shouting orders. I lowered my face just an inch, and there was Jenny. She tasted as good as she smelled.

Guns thundered on both sides, and I let them have at it. "Got me another'n!" somebody said.

Then it was quiet. A breeze had come up and its coolness cleared the reek of gunpowder and whispered on the flats. The pit fires danced beyond their mounds. Distant, muted voices and the scuffle of animals milling about the enclave. The air cold and Jenny warm against me . . .

"Well, did he?" someone asked.

"Did he what?" another voice answered in the darkness.

"Did he kiss her?"

"I believe he did," someone else said.

And there was another sound that came with the glow of a dim lantern . . . the sound of someone scribbling on paper. I damn near brained myself on the trestle beam coming up under that wagon. "Artemis Steen," I yelled. "If you write another word I'll brain you."

CHAPTER SIXTEEN

The morning that came, when it finally did, was grey and sad. Rob Simpson was dead, out on the flats where he had been guarding the stock. Bennie Quinn had a bullet through his leg and several of the men had nicks and scratches.

Most of the draft stock had been saved, but at least two were dead and quite a few scattered. They wouldn't go far, but it would take another day to bring them in. We found three dead raiders, that was all. It hadn't been much of an attack, really, more harassment than an all-out raid, and we wondered at that.

"They want us to move," Billy suggested. "They intend to drive us on to Camden Cut."

"Well, they've done it," Chapman growled. "We can't stay here. They'll just come back and cut us to pieces."

We couldn't go back, either. At least here the terrain had worked for us. Places east, we wouldn't even have that advantage. A wagon train on the move is a formidable thing, and no easy target when it is rolling. But trains have to stop. Stock has to graze. People have to rest. Gear has to be mended. A wagon train at rest is defensible against casual hostility. But it is no fortress.

We all talked it around and around, but there wasn't any other answer. We had to go on.

The one slight advantage we had was that they

didn't know we knew they were waiting at Camden Road Cut. They knew we were scouting, just like we knew they were watching us. But they didn't know about Billy Hawk. There weren't many who could have made that long scout and found the outlaw's nest and made it back again, without ever being seen.

"They intend to ambush us, then?" Artemis Steen was taking it all in. "At that wash Mr. Hawthorne described?"

"It's more than a wash," Billy said. "It's big. More like a gorge."

Steen started to write something and then stopped. "Ah, the burden of the semanticist." He shook his head. "Great events unfold upon a new land, and the vernacular at hand is not equal to the reporting of them. Is it dry?"

"What? The gorge? Yes, at this season. Why?"

"A phrase is needed, blending the drama of impending ambush with the complexities of terrain. New frontiers require new vocabularies, you know."

"They do?" Hazen cocked his head.

"Absolutely. Yet one cannot say that those gentlemen intend, upon our arrival there, to *gorge* us. It simply won't do. No." He started writing again, satisfied. "We are to be dry-washed."

"History in the making," Billy Hawk said.

"If it ever gets out," I said, "nobody will ever believe it."

"Sure they will," Hazen said. "It'll be in all the newspapers."

Mason Chapman, bleak and bothered, standing in the midst of his sad, shot-up wagon assemblage, shook his head and rubbed a big hand across his eyes. "You're all crazy."

There was burying to do and stock to round up. Stanley Simpson and his family took in Rob Simpson's widow, and one of the bachelors, H.T. Putney, took charge of her wagon for her.

We had to move. They could come again, and if ever they got our herd, we would be defenseless and stranded. With guards out in strength we had a strategy meeting. Mason Chapman had Billy Hawk describe again the layout at Camden Road Cut. "You sure they didn't see you?"

The Indian took off his hat, raven hair glistening in the late sun. "Of course they didn't," he said.

He had counted about thirty. They were border ruffians mostly, renegades who roamed western Missouri like wolf packs, preying on the defenseless. A few, Billy thought, were of a different cut, pure outlaws of the kind who ran with Quantrill, Anderson, and Baker.

"Did you see Mark Hayden?" Chapman asked.

"No. But I did see Walt Murray. He was the only one I recognized."

"You got in that close that you could see faces," Hazen said, and there was a look on his face of dawning recognition. He stared at Billy like he'd seen a ghost. "I know you. I thought I'd seen you before. Then just now, when you took off your hat . . ." He looked around at the rest of us. "When Captain Nevers called up the militia at Freeport he hired Potawatomi scouts. He brought in a Delaware to teach them how." He looked back at Billy, his eyes big. "That was you."

"Sure," the Indian said. "I know that."

"But you died!" Hazen insisted. "I remember! At Dover Cross two of Striker's men cornered you in a barn. You all killed each other."

Billy grinned that evil grin of his. "Doesn't seem

that way, does it?"

Chapman said, "There were three of them, Hazen, not two. And one of them was an Indian. That's who died at Dover Cross."

Artemis Steen had a fresh pad out and was scribbling notes. It looked like another legend was in the making.

As dusk fell some of the other men joined us there. They all knew now that there was no avoiding the outlaws ahead. There would be more fighting and shooting, and the only thing between their families and those roaring guns would be a sheet of canvas and two or three inches of seasoned wood.

Asa stared dismally into the firelight. "I got to turn back. I can't take Peggy and the kids any further."

Several others nodded. Bert Sutherland added, "Only thing to do. There's no land for us, anyway."

Jed O'Hannon set the butt of his rifle on the ground. "Won't do any good to turn back," he said. "We've already talked about that. It never would have done any good. Those are horsemen out there. They can cover thirty miles while we cover six or seven. If we go ahead we face them at that cut. If we stay here they'll come at us like last night, and if we turn back they'll have us strung out in the woods for days and just pick us off. I don't know what's best."

Jenny Sutton came into the light then, along with several other women. She was wearing boys' clothes again, and carrying Joey's old cylinder rifle. The other women had guns, too—rifles, muskets, shotguns, an old dueling pistol, and one carried a blunderbuss that must have been eighty years old.

Grace O'Hannon spoke for the delegation. "We didn't come this far to turn back now, Asa. None of us did. So you men get that out of your heads. You just decide what we're going to do and then let's get about it. But no more talk of turning back. We've come too far for that."

Of a sudden I had an image of the creek cut ahead, and of men on the rises firing down into wagons full of women and children. Jenny would be in one of those wagons. She must have read what I was thinking. She said, "I can shoot near as well as you, Jeremy Burke. We all can."

I guess there isn't anything as independent as a dependent female. Right then in the whole wide world there wasn't anybody was going to get those women out of there safely unless it was us. And they knew that, and just plain assumed we would come up with a way . . . never doubted it for a minute. Just wanted to make it clear to us that whatever way we came up with to save all our bacons had better be their way.

"What we have here," Hazen Burnett pointed out, "is a situation."

"Any ideas?" Chapman asked.

Billy Hawk was scratching his head. "One way to turn a disadvantage on the field is to take the offense. Trouble is, a wagon train is equipped only for defense. Lot of guns, good field of fire, but a train is slow and highly visible and there's no way to camouflage it. Then again, I've been watching this train the times we've traveled in Jeremy's phalanx order, and it reminds me of something."

"What's that?"

"A ship of the line."

I've always heard that Indians are inscrutable. I never tried to scrute one, but I guess that is right because William Hawthorne, the noble savage, had me baffled right then. Somebody needed to say,

"Ship of the line?" So I did.

"There are similarities," Billy said. "A ship of the line is big and clumsy and heavily armed and it can't hide. It's a battleship. Its whole purpose is to bring a lot of guns to bear at a critical point. Look at this train in rows of three, closed up. It is a dreadnought, taken as a unit. The problem is, how to get it into action as an offensive weapon."

Mason Chapman just stared at him. "You mean attack them? With a wagon train?" At Billy's nod Chapman's mouth dropped open even further. "Billy, you can't *attack* somebody with a wagon train. That ain't what wagon trains are for."

"I saw a man attack a fellow with a sack of manure once," Hazen tossed in. "That wasn't what it was for, either, but he knocked the fellow down with it."

"Nobody expects to be attacked with a sack of manure," Chapman chided.

"My point exactly," Billy Hawk said. "Or a wagon train."

"It can't be done," Chapman said.

"Then let's hear a better idea."

In the silence that followed I was thinking along some strange lines. "I wonder," I wondered aloud, "whether anybody on this train has a bugle?"

We didn't come up with a plan, as plans go, that night, but the seeds had been sown for some original thinking.

Where we sat now, it was just two long days to Camden Road Cut. The last place fit for a defense, Billy said, was a hogback ridge just two miles from the cut where the woods had been burned over. "Can we time it to be there, Mason, if we push it?"

"We can try," Chapman said.

The train had to move. We had to drive by day

and be ready to defend by night. That night raid on us had left no choice. Still, they had suffered some and might hesitate to try it again right now. And it might just keep the yayhoos off their guard to see us rushing right into their net that obligingly.

At first light we were up and rolling, and for the first mile or two while the open prairie held we strung the wagons out in a long front, rolling side by side in a line several hundred yards across with a bunch of us on horseback forming a sort of flying wedge out front.

I was wishing we would encounter some of those hooraws that way, out here in broad daylight on open ground, just to see how they would handle a situation like that. But they never showed up. Oh, they were watching, all right, and we could imagine the head-scratching back at the nest when word came in about this latest formation.

By noon, though, we were in rough country again and only managing our phalanx at intervals. Sometimes in those breaks we were strung out a half mile, and it took all the riding Hazen and I could do to keep guns out on the flanks. Billy stayed out ahead where he was best.

It had turned out there was a bugle on the train. Old Mr. Tetherstall had one that he had carried back when the Second Connecticut went to guard Baltimore during the depression. Mrs. Tetherstall kept it packed away in a trunk so he couldn't play with it. Seemed the last time he had blown it was at a Presbyterian church funeral and nobody had known in advance that he was going to.

"Can you play a cavalry charge on it?" I asked him.

"I don't know. I was infantry. But I can play reveille and taps."

"Well, how about 'Riders Up?' Or 'Boots and Saddles'?"

"I don't known any of those," he confessed. "But I can play 'Come To The Bower' pretty good, and 'Sweet Molly's Drawers,' and I've turned a hand to 'Requiem For A Lost Lark' on occasion. Would any of those do?"

"Well, don't play it now," I urged him. "I'll give it some thought."

I kept thinking about my old buddies Grizzly and Skinny, who might be among the citizens up there in Camden Road Cut.

We sorely needed a plan.

That became more obvious as the day wore on. The rough lands to both sides closed in here, like a funnel with us in it, narrowing toward the creek cut. The real badlands were still ahead, but these here were bad enough.

I met Billy out ahead for a better look. "You see what I mean," he said. "There's only one place we can cross."

"Do you have a plan for what we do next?"

"Well, it's not much of a plan. But I have a notion."

"So do I."

If I was counting right, we could mount twenty-two grown men able to ride and carry a gun. But that would almost deplete the train. My vague notions about diversion and surprise attack were fine as far as they went, but they had no substance to them. I just couldn't bring the whole picture together. "What was that about you leaving three men dead at Freeport?" I asked him.

"I've done a lot of things," he said, being inscrutable again.

We made our ten miles that day, and it was the

longest drive of the passage. When we ringed the wagons in the evening, with the stock in a ridge pocket where they could be guarded, we were a tired bunch of people. And all eyes kept turning nervously to the west. We were only a day now from Camden Road Cut.

We met together around coffee pots while there still was light in the sky, so that everybody could be there when we talked. As they gathered I knelt beside Billy Hawk at the fire. "Where you found those men . . . could you lead a bunch of us there without us being seen?"

He thought it over. "Maybe. On foot."

"Then maybe we can surprise them."

"They'll be watching us, Jeremy. If we stop here, if we pull off a lot of men, they'll know we've spotted them. We'll lose the advantage."

Others had gathered around. Jenny Sutton said, "Then don't stop the train."

"We haven't enough men to keep it going and send out an attack party," Chapman said. "Sure, the women could drive, but they'd see. They'd know the men were gone. Then they'd come for the train."

Jenny said, "Not if a lot of women were dressed as men."

Grace O'Hannon turned away, her back straight. "Come along, ladies, let's see what we can find that fits."

Chapman looked after them, distressed. "But we haven't made a plan yet."

"As far as those women are concerned," Burnett said, "we have."

In the dark before dawn, with lanterns dead and the fires down to coals, twenty-two of us saddled up in the cove where the stock was kept. Some of the women came to help, and Jenny clung to me like she couldn't stand it, but her voice in the darkness was brave.

"Don't worry, Jeremy," she said. "It's going to be all right. You'll see."

And suddenly I had my arms around her, without knowing how they'd got there. "I'm glad I kissed you back there," I told her. To prove it, I did it again.

Twenty-two of us slipped away from the camp in darkness, on quiet mounts, and lit for the woods north of the trail, Billy Hawk in the lead.

Mason Chapman had assured us, "These wagons will roll at dawn, and they'll look the same as always. You boys just take care of yourselves."

Could a bunch of women drive those big wagons in close phalanx? Thinking on it, I decided those women could do about anything they turned their hands to.

We put distance between us and the wagons, past the crests where spotters might be. Then while it was still full dark we lined out west, picking our way through woods and hills as faint grey unfolded around us.

About now, we knew, a few men and a bunch of determined women and kids were making up the train for a day's march, getting the hitching done while it was still too dark for anyone to see that that was all they were. They would move and Mason Chapman would be counting the wheel turns and watching the sun, making time to spare and then sparing it carefully so that the train would arrive at a precise point just at dusk—a place visibly defensible by armed men with wagons, at a time when spotters might not see that the armed men were gone.

They would be vulnerable then, those women and kids, and we would not be there to defend them. Only darkness and diversion could do that, and Mason Chapman's mastery of the movement of trains.

We had a plan now, and it was a harebrained plan but it had to work. It just had to.

We spelled the horses for a half-hour at midmorning in a little triangle valley where flowers poked through the winter grass. At noon we paused for a cold meal on a hillside, and late in the afternoon we came up on a ridge where cedars climbed from the hardwood bottoms toward a bare knob that was a landmark. Billy went on ahead, and when he came back he said, "Picket the horses. We go from here afoot."

Only two animals remained saddled, and their riders, old Mr. Tetherstall and the younger Hollings boy, Chet, sat them nervously, watching the rest of us shoulder our gear. Chet Hollings carried a rifle and had two pistols strapped to his saddle. Mr. Tetherstall carried his bugle.

"You know your route now," Billy Hawk told them. "You can get your horses across the gorge where you see a pair of bare ridges with a stand of cedars below them. Go on west to the next crest and make cold camp." He eyed the Hollings boy intently. "You sure you can reckon the time in the morning?"

The boy didn't falter. "I can reckon it."

"Good. Then from your camp it is south to the trail, then east a mile. The marks are like we talked about."

Mr. Tetherstall looked at his bugle and licked his lips. "I ought to practice," he said.

"No practice," I warned him. "Not a sound. But

when it's time to blow, you give 'er hell."

They rode away, angling north as Billy had pointed them, and we set out afoot.

It was almost dark when we came to a high drop-off, a canyon that was an oversized gully with sheer sides and a ribbon of water in the bottom. I moved up with Billy. "Camden Road Cut?"

He pointed downstream. "Half a mile," he said quietly.

As the men came up I told them, "Get some rest here, but be quiet. Sounds carry."

Billy Hawk dumped his gear. "Jeremy, Hazen, let's go look."

The vantage point Billy found was a patch of brush right at the top of the cut on the east bank, where a tree had fallen and vines had taken it over. We wormed through there and found ourselves twenty feet above the heads of six men lazing around a campfire. The air was rich with rising smoke and the smell of roasting meat. There was another fire a ways off in the bottom of the draw, and a third one on the far bank, on a shelf just below the crest.

As we watched, someone set a small fire on down the canyon, where more men gathered. Further down, beyond that, were a couple of dark sheds, barely visible in the dusk. They were just past the incline of a sloping shelf that cut upward into the sheer canyon wall. That would be Camden Road Cut, where the wagons must cross.

Someone knelt at the second fire to pour coffee from a pot and I recognized him. It was Walt Murray.

We watched for a while, scarcely daring to breath. Then we eased away, backed off into the brush and compared what we had seen. Beyond the campsites, horses were held in a roped-off section of the gully. The gully's bottom was a maze of shale tumbles, breaks, and crevices, not at all like a smooth wash. We couldn't count the men down there, but there were plenty. It was, as Billy had said, a real outlaw's nest.

Billy guessed they would have about four sentinels out, and he pointed out where he figured they would be.

Seeing it now, the actual place where we must meet, the whole plan we had worked so hard on seemed awfully flimsy. We crept away and went back to where the others were waiting.

We were a sorry lot, huddled out there in the cold darkness of western Missouri, face to face with the reality of a plan that had sounded pretty good at the time.

"It isn't going to work," Hazen said dismally. "There are too many of them and they're scattered all up and down that gulch. Our plan is shot to hell."

"What is the plan, anyway?" one of them asked, and I realized that most of them hadn't known exactly what we were up to even when we were up to it. Most of them had been too busy back there, worrying about their families, to be in on the planning.

"What we had contemplated," Billy Hawk said, "was a hammer-and-anvil strike."

"We figured we could get ourselves stationed along that west rim," I added, "and open up on that bunch just at the right time to get their whole attention on us. Then the wagons would top out on the east rim and spread into a firing front and nail them from there. We'd have them in a crossfire, with the element of surprise on our side, and we could take the fight out of them before they ever got started."

"Like a hammer and an anvil," Hazen continued. "Us being the anvil and the train being the hammer."

They thought about it, and Jobe Gurley asked, "So what's wrong with the plan? Can't we go ahead and do that?"

Billy shook his head, a long-haired silhouette in the darkness. "We had hoped they would be concentrated under our fire. They aren't. They're spread out along a couple of hundred yards down there, and they've got good cover. We'd never be able to contain them. They'd scatter, get to their horses and there we'd be, afoot. They'd wipe us out."

"And then take the train," Hazen added.

"And then take the train," Billy agreed.

There was a long silence. Then one of the young Fiser brothers asked, innocently, "Well, why don't we get their horses first?"

There was more silence after that. Finally Hazen said, "Well, why don't we?"

"We could do that," Billy replied. "And I guess we could make them pay a price. But we still can't set up the crossfire, and we can't protect the wagons without it."

"We can't win, then?" someone asked.

"If we can't win, we lose."

We had the advantage of surprise, but they had the advantage of terrain in a way we couldn't have foreseen. That wasn't one coordinated gang down there; that was several small bunches, and they kept aloof from one another except when the fighting came. That wasn't one camp; it was several. We could still attack, and maybe cut the odds. But there were hardcases down there who wouldn't be buffaloed for long. Even if we succeeded, a lot of us would die. And they would still be around to take the wagons . . . at least some of them would.

What would be nice, I allowed, was if all those men down there were lumped together in one place, in the open canyon bottom right at the cut, when the wagons topped out.

Hazen sounded like he was being patient with a yayhoo on yodelberries. "That would be convenient," he drawled, "but it just ain't the case."

"But if we don't have our hammer-and-anvil then we don't have anything. Seems to me the only thing really wrong is those hooraws are spread too thin. Maybe we could bunch the herd some way."

"I concur with your hypothesis." Hazen's voice sounded discouraged. "Only one thing. How do we get them to do that?"

"I don't know," I admitted. "Hell, I have a couple of passing acquaintances down there. Maybe I could get everybody to gather 'round so I can tell them the one about Willie McBride and his homing chicken. I don't know."

Probably most of them then concurred with the hypothesis that I was on yodelberries. But the Indian was interested. "Maybe you're talking sense, Jeremy. You don't sound like you are, but then you never do. Do you think you could get into that camp?"

"Oh, I could get in, all right. After all, I'm a Hoosier and a pistol prodigy. But then what?"

"Talk to 'em," Hazen offered, sounding interested, too. "Maybe somebody down there has a hydrophoby bug."

"Or be interested in how to mine pearls," someone else said.

"Or the fine art of bumping into ladies," Hazen

213

added.

"You're crazy! You're all crazy."

"It ain't us that's fixing to go down there and tell tall tales to thirty-eleven outlaws," one of them argued.

"I didn't say I was going to do that."

"Well, you didn't say you wasn't."

"What's that about a homing chicken?" somebody asked. "I haven't ever heard that one."

It is just amazing how many people haven't heard that story.

"The rest of us will go for the horses," Hazen said.

"And after you get them all together we will anvil the hell out of them," Will Fiser added, enthusiastic now that everything was arranged.

Hazen turned serious, then. "Billy, you said they'd have four sentries out. That means two of them on the east cut, where the wagons are coming in. Can you take them out?"

I could make out Billy Hawk's white teeth grinning in the darkness, and the glint of starlight on a drawn knife blade. "Gladly," he said.

"I'm not going down there," I insisted. "I don't know any way to get them bunched up."

"You'll think of something," Hazen assured me. "And anyway, everybody likes to get a look at a living legend."

CHAPTER SEVENTEEN

Sure, I'd think of something.

Pa always used to say a man is at his best when the chips are down and the hands are spread, because that's the only point in the game that the decision is simple. Either pick up your winnings or shoot out the light.

I would think of something.

I was working on it all the way down that dark bluff to the bottom of the gorge, and all the way across, ducking in the darkness so no firelight from the outlaws' camps below might show me to them. I was working on it while I climbed the west bluff and all the way along that blufftop to where I could hear their muffled snores in the canyon below me. I was working on it as I crouched on a shale ledge right over the head of one of their sentries. I had to think of something.

Trouble was, even when I stood again on the canyon floor, folding that sentry over so his boots wouldn't show around the shoulder of rock, I still hadn't thought of anything. And a little later, when I was directly across the stream from the first fire and trying not to make any noise while I stuffed another yayhoo down into a crack in the low shelf, I still hadn't thought of anything then, either.

As far as I could tell, that accounted for everybody who was awake up at this end of the camp. But judging by the grey in the sky above the east rim, there would be others stirring soon.

All the fires that I could see were down to coals, a ragged string of red glows winding off along the floor and shelves of the gorge for a couple of hundred yards or more. These fellows hadn't been here long and they didn't intend to stay long. They were wasting firewood like it didn't matter, keeping all these separate fires just to keep their distance from one another. Not that I blamed them. If I had taken to consorting with yayhoos I wouldn't want to get too close, either.

Thinking about yayhoos reminded me of my pair of old trail buddies from the woods. Grizzly and Skinny.

There was a little time yet before anything really needed to happen, so I went looking for them. At the first fire I tossed some tinder on the coals and looked at the faces sleeping there. One of them was covered up in his blankets and I had to lift the corner to see, and it wasn't anybody I knew. He snorted and muttered, "Wha'ya want?"

"Sorry, wrong camp." I dropped the blanket back over him. Then, since nobody else seemed to be noticing, I whopped him on the head with a rock. When you haven't got a plan, you just do what comes handy.

I started to move on and another one there rose up out of his blankets. "What you want here?" he griped.

"Sorry," I said. "I got lost. Lookin' for a place to pee."

"Well, go on downstream someplace. And stay away from the creek. We need the water for coffee." As I moved off he rolled down into his blankets again and muttered, "Knothead."

The third fire I checked, almost to the silt fan

where the trail cut through the gorge, sure enough, there was Grizzly. There were five of them at the fire. I stoked it up and tapped him on the shoulder. He sputtered and blinked and sat up. "Is it time?"

"I don't think so." I grinned at him. "Howdy. I see you boys got here all right. You got any coffee?"

He stared at me. "Oh, it's you. The pistol prodigy. Make your own coffee, dumb-ass. We ain't got any to spare."

Another one had come awake to see what was going on, and it was good old Skinny. "Hey there," I said. "Good to see you again."

"The Hoosier," he said, sourly. "The blesset same one. We prob'ly gonna cut you open, you damn showoff."

"Oh? Why's that?"

"Because you made us out a couple of fools, is why."

"All that about cavalry and bugles," Grizzly added. "We nigh busted down two good horses gettin' here to spread the word, and there wasn't no cavalry. Why'd you say a thing like that?"

"I'm pretty sure there was," I told him. The most convincing thing there is is sincerity. Once you can fake that, you got it made.

The other three were stirring now, and one of them said, "Is this the one?"

"The very one. He's one of them pistol paladin prodigies the newspapers talk about."

"That so? Lord, it's gettin' so half the yayhoos you meet are one of them."

"Here's some coffee." I found a pot still half full and set it on the fire. "What's the schedule?"

Grizzly squinted up at the greying sky. "Come morning, they either be here or we go out and get them."

"Lot of money on that train," Skinny said. "And women, too. We gonna have some fun and get rich."

"Not if those cavalry get here first."

The last of the five was right beside where I was squatted, and he stirred a little bit, laid back the corner of his blanket roll, and then did a fast turn upright and stuck a gun barrel right under my chin. "Hee-hee-hee," he cackled, "I thought I heard home folks. Howdy there Jeremy."

I had been coming right along until then. Now my heart sank right down into the seat of my britches. Of all the rotten, stinking luck.

"Aw, crap," I said, "I haven't got time for you right now, Joshua."

It was light enough to see clearly when they hauled me up on the rise of the silt bank, and the gorge wasn't full of sleepy campsites anymore. They were all up and wide awake and raring to see the living legend before I became a dead legend.

Joshua Sutton kept buzzing around wanting to shoot me or stick me or brain me, but the rest of them held him off while somebody went over and started rapping on the slab door of the shack. My hands were tied behind me and Joshua Sutton had my Walker stuck in his belt. The damn fool. It was full-loaded and he didn't know anything about Walkers. If it took a notion to mash the cap he probably had its hammer setting on, it would geld him. Joshua never did have the brains God gave a goose.

I kept being looked at and commented about. "You mean this is the real one? Like in the newspapers?" "This is the one that took out Fred and Marvin back there?" "Hell, he don't look like anything but a Hoosier." "What's a Hoosier?" Like that.

Joshua Sutton busted through the crowd and

tried to stab me in the stomach with a long knife, and I had to shy to one side to evade him. I planted a knee in his belly as he went by, hoping that Walker would go off and change his perspective, but it didn't. All he did was fold over and vomit.

Somebody took the knife away from him, and when he got his breath he wiped his face on his coat sleeve and walked over and stared at me with eyes like a snake. "I'm gonna kill you slow," he whispered. Then he hauled off and punched me in the belly. It doubled me over, but some of them were holding me so I didn't fall.

"Leave him alone 'til the boss sees him," one of them said.

"He's mine," Joshua said. "I came to kill him and that's what I'm going to do."

"Joshua," I managed to say, "don't you know your sister is on that wagon train? Your sister!"

Those snake eyes never changed, and I could tell Joshua had never changed any. He always had been the plain stupid meanest yayhoo I ever saw. He still was. "That's her lookout. I ain't her mother."

And he meant it. He didn't care, not a whit. I shook my head. "Joshua, they should have drowned you when you were weaned." That made him flare and step forward so I could kick him in the belly again. That damned Walker still didn't go off. But that time Joshua stayed where he fell.

It was almost full morning, and all through it I had kept listening. There would be a signal of some kind, I was sure. I knew there weren't any east sentries out there where there had been. Billy Hawk was very thorough about things like that. But it seemed likely there would be spotters out on the crest over the trail, and they would signal when they spotted the wagons, so the sentries could relay it.

Also, I was still trying to think up a plan. I had been thinking so hard, for so long, about how to get the whole tribe bunched up here in the middle that it didn't dawn on me for a while that I didn't need to think about that anymore. That was already taken care of. The problem was, so was I.

Pa always said he figured dying was like being born. It didn't matter how you felt about it, it just happened anyway. I didn't guess I'd see the rest of it. Somehow, maybe Hazen and Billy and the rest could bring it off, just as we'd planned. Maybe the wagons and the people who were what mattered could be saved from this bunch. Maybe. I just sorely wished I could have had a hand in the doing of it.

I heard sounds from over by the shack, and a minute later Mark Hayden, Luther Fritch, and Walt Murray pushed through the crowd. They stopped when they saw me, and just stared.

"It *is* him," Fritch growled. Walt Murray got a gleam in his eyes like the delights of hell, and stepped up and hit me so hard the world spun and I found myself lying flat on my face and chewing on sand.

". . . kill the son-of-a-bitch," somebody was saying, far off. ". . . peel the hide off him . . ."
". . . need to know what he's doing here . . ."
". . . hole in his belly and leave him there . . ."
Even farther off, way out in the real world, there was an owl hoot. And then another. But those weren't owls. I was hurting so bad I felt like I was all busted up, but suddenly I knew it was time. Those had been the spotters. The train was moving in. I was the only one there who paid any mind to the distant sounds. They were expecting their sentries to bring the message in. But they didn't have any sentries. They didn't know about Billy Hawk.

But I did. I knew several things they didn't know. Lying there with my face in the dirt I started grinning, and the blood in my mouth had the sweet taste of retribution.

All I was supposed to do was gather them in one place. It was done. The herd was bunched. And with my head on the ground I could hear the thunder of running horses.

Hard hands hauled me upright, and I shook my head to clear it. Mark Hayden was there, and he tipped back his head to look down his nose at me. "All right, Burke, I want some answers."

Luther Fritch stepped in between us, peering hard at my face. It must have been a sight, but he cocked his head. "What are you grinning about?"

I looked right past him at Hayden. "Because you've lost," I told him.

The sound grew then like thunder rolling, and heads turned toward it. Men yelled and gunfire rang out, and I heard a high-pitched "yip-yip-yip!" through the din. A hunter's yell. The riders came at a run, right through us, guns blazing as they rode us down. Men scattered, turned to fire, and were bounced aside. I swung around, pulling loose from the men who held me, and butted one of them with my head. Then something hit me from behind and I rolled clear over him, hit the ground and came up shoulders down against a claybank, so dazed I didn't know where I was for a minute.

By the time I got my eyes to working a few of the riders were topping out on the west cut and others were spreading out along the top of the cliff and starting to shoot down among us.

A few of the boys had gone on through, up the canyon, and they were circling up there above the camp, firing back toward the cut. Down below, there were others behind rocks, shooting.

The outlaws were scurrying around in confusion, but not for long. There were crevices and rocks, and they began finding cover and shooting back.

"Jeremy!" somebody yelled. "Over here!"

I saw a hat wave. Somebody was under the west rim, down behind a shale-fall, signaling me. I got my legs under me and ran like I never ran before.

When I was a kid I always figured that when it rained you could stay dry if you could just run fast enough to go between the raindrops. It never worked, but I was always trying it. I'm glad I had that practice. Somehow I got across that creek and up the west shelf and dived in behind that shale-fall without getting hit. I'm pretty sure I ran between the bullets.

"You look like hell," Hazen Burnett said.

There were three of them there, Hazen and the two older Thompkins brothers. One of them cut me loose and the other one said, "Where's your gun?"

"I lost it."

"Well, you can't do any good here without a gun. This is a gunfight we're having."

I had about forgotten how really narrow-minded Sidney Thompkins could be.

"You bunched them pretty good," Hazen said. "I knew you'd think of something. Problem now is how are we going to keep them bunched? You see that?" He paused to squeeze off a shot, and ducked as a ball spanged shale behind us. "They're starting to scatter again. We got men above and below, but there aren't enough of us to hold them."

"Where's that battleship?" Sidney Thompkins asked.

"Where's that what?"

"Battleship. That Indian said them wagons is a

battleship. Where is it?"

"Tell the truth," his brother said, popping up to shoot at somebody, "I think that Indian is crazy."

I raised up for a look. I guess after that horse charge, and all the shooting and havoc in the canyon, I expected to see quite a few dead bodies. But I could only count three men down out there. Pa used to say a gun battle is usually more gun than battle. A lot more people know how to shoot than know how to hit. And I was acutely aware that most of this brave crew of ours was just a bunch of farmers.

One of the three men down was Joshua. I pointed. "There's my gun."

"Do you want to go get it?"

"I guess I'd better."

"Wait a minute." Hazen was reloading his revolver. "Okay," he said. "Go."

When I came up from the fall a man out by the creek raised up to shoot at me and I heard Hazen's Colt talking. The man went down. It was a long thirty yards to where Joshua lay, but I got there and dropped down beside him. He was trying to crawl off but not quite up to it yet. I pushed him down and rolled him over. "Lay still," I said. "You want to get killed?"

The Walker was still in his belt and it was an awful temptation, but I just pulled it out. Just like I suspected, he had its hammer resting on a live round. It was only by the grace of God that he still had his essentials.

A ball whipped past my ear and I swatted Joshua down again. "I said lay still."

By rolling once I got down into a shallow depression, just about a foot deep, then dragged Joshua in after me. "Now just for once in your life," I told him, "behave yourself."

I left him there. The only direction I could move from here was down toward the creek, so I crawled down that way, poking up after I was under good cover. I found I was almost at the top of the shelf, and even as I looked a gun went off almost in my ear and powder burned my face. I didn't even look to see who it was. He had come up not three feet from me, and the Walker's shot sent him cartwheeling backward to fall half over the shelf's edge. It was Walt Murray.

And I was right in the middle of them. A ball scattered dust over me. Another tugged at my sleeve. I lunged and dived headfirst over the shelf. I hit and slid and the Walker was wrenched out of my hand. I came up and ran headlong into Luther Fritch.

I had always suspected he wasn't really fat. He wasn't. I bounced off a body as solid as a market hog, and he swung and hit me alongside the head with a blow that made red fog hang there for an instant. I saw the next one coming and blocked it, then put all the power I had into a single punch, square to the face. I didn't have time for more than one. Somebody else was at my back. A hand holding a gun swung at my head and glanced across my shoulder. I took the arm as it came across and broke it.

I was windmilling, but it was all I could think of to do. I was square in the middle of a bunch of them. I whirled and backhanded a face that was there and flipped him backward over a rock, then wanted to go after him because it was Mark Hayden, but I didn't have time. Two others were coming around the shelf with guns in their hands. I dived and rolled and came up with the Walker.

"Don't!" Grizzly yelled and raised his hands. Skinny bumped into him from behind and fell down and Grizzly tripped over him. They disappeared back around the shelf. Some folks really do believe everything they read.

Mark Hayden was gone. There was shooting from the west rim, and sporadic shooting from cover on the canyon floor, and it looked like the boys were holding them. Then I saw Hayden. He was running up the east slope, and then he stopped, looked around, and I noticed I had messed up his face for him, at least. He looked west, then both ways along the canyon, and I saw what he saw. His men were boxed three ways, but the east slope was open. And he knew with all of us down here the approaching wagon train was undefended.

"Here!" he yelled, waving his arms. "All of you, to me!"

And I knew they could do it. A rush back to the east slope, a retreat up it, getting out of our range, and they'd have us boxed down here and on the other side. The whole plan fell apart right before my eyes. They could make it. They could get above us, and they could take the wagons. Then they could start a systematic killing that wouldn't stop until we were dead. And we were not in position to stop them.

I got my feet under me and braced the Walker with both hands and held on Mark Hayden's distant figure and . . . something hit me behind the knees and I went over backward. One of the men I had knocked down was up and fighting. He took the shot I had meant for Hayden.

But I had lost the chance. They had heard his call, and they were moving, from all sides, back to join him and escape our trap. I busted one with a shot, clipped another, tried to line on a third and lost him in the shale. It was too late. The wagons . . . Jenny . . .

I shot again, but it was a futile thing. They were a

mass again, with a leader, and they arrowed toward the east slope. The Walker's hammer fell on an empty chamber.

I stood there without hope, and heard the sudden silence of defeat.

Then, ringing clear in the morning air, came the distant, martial call of a bugle. It rang distant and it rang near as the canyon walls caught it and echoed its call.

The funneling mass of men stopped in its tracks, and heads turned in bewilderment. The call grew to klaxon clarity and the walls resounded it.

"Oh, my God," someone shouted. "He was right! That's a bugle!"

"Cavalry!" someone else hollered.

"Which way?"

"Hell, I don't know! I can't tell! Let's get out of here!"

Like sand on a marble, they scattered, most of them running blind, in panic. Confused and bewildered, they ran, some of them in circles, some blindly away, and our boys closed the anvil's arm and its holding jaws to contain them. There was gunfire again, and now it was mostly ours and mostly organized. They closed and the milling mob tightened and I ran, reloading as I went, to come up on them from the creek while Hazen and the men came down on them from the bluffs.

Now it was all out in the open, and furious. Desperate return fire came from the outlaws as we closed. And there were still as many of them as of us, and they started to see that.

In that moment I heard the bull voice of Mason Chapman, bless his soul, ring out, "All you men! Stand and deliver!"

Now where he got that selection of words I'll

never know, but that's what it occurred to him to say, and he said it, and it did its job. Everybody froze, right where they were.

I had come right up into them, and I looked around and it looked like a French town meeting. There were twenty shocked, armed men around me, and among them were men on the ground. Beyond, coming off the west bluff, was a grim line of settlers with hot and fresh-loaded rifles. And up on the east bank were wagons, drawn up in attack formation, a phalanx spread for assault, a many-wheeled ship of the line with guns poking out all over. There was one wagon right in the cut, and Mason Chapman stood on its box, a scattergun at his cheek, looking as ominous as a man can look.

One of the outlaws broke and lit for the cover of the east bank, and was almost at the top when Billy Hawk appeared there, knife in hand and a grin on his face. The knife flashed in the sunlight.

I was looking at all that when I heard Asa, somewhere to my left, call out, "Jeremy! Watch yourself!" and a gun went off directly behind me. The blow in my side turned me halfway around, and even as I stumbled there was another shot, high up, from atop the wagon bank above the cut. I straightened and turned, and Joshua Sutton was standing there, a gun in his hand and a hole in his head. He toppled as I saw him, and I was about to. The shock of being shot was setting in. I looked up at the top of the cut. A slim, graceful form in boys' clothes stood there, a wisp of smoke curling from the old revolving rifle she held. Even up there against the morning I noticed how pale her face was, how large her eyes.

CHAPTER EIGHTEEN

Mr. Abercrombie was dead. So was Sammy Thompkins. So was Orlo Fiser, who had caught a knife wielded by an outlaw who came up behind him. That outlaw didn't ever knife another man. Fiser's two grown sons saw to that.

A lot of our bunch had cuts and scrapes, and Artemis Steen had a knot on his head almost the size of his head.

The hole in my side bled a good bit but my guts weren't leaking. Billy Hawk tended me with a hot axe head and some of that mustard-smelling poultice that he carried for special occasions. I'd like to have died from him repairing me, but I did feel better afterward.

Several of the bandits didn't ever leave that Camden Road canyon. The ground down in the bottoms was softer to dig than the ground up on top, so they buried them down there where they fell. Of the thirty-seven in Mark Hayden's gang twelve were dead, four were badly hurt, and a dozen or so had walking wounds.

They found the preacher, John Thomas Reazin, hiding in a brush tumble down canyon, babbling with fright. They looked for Hayden, but couldn't find him. He was gone.

The settlers had a council. Some were for hanging the lot of them and some were for shooting them. They compromised.

They pulled out two wagons—Hayden's and Fritch's—loaded the injured men into them, stripped the whole gang of weapons and set them to marching east, defenseless through a country fairly crawling with yayhoos just like them.

"Biblical justice," O'Hannon declared it.

They said Jenny was took down with the shakes pretty bad for a day or so, but I didn't know. I was asleep, because I had a hole in me.

I slept most of the way to the Grand River.

Nobody ever tamed the north route crossing of the Grand. Some times of the year it couldn't be crossed at all. Other times you crossed it the way we did. The men cut timbers and built winches and A-frames, and set to work.

It took four days to get our train across the Grand, and there were some close calls, but Mason Chapman knew how to get us there and he had a seasoned bunch of folks now to work with.

On high ground west of the Grand we spent a day in camp to make repairs. There were axles to brace, harness straps to mend, horses to be shod, and clothes to be washed. Some of the boys roasted a whole beef over a pit.

I was managing to be up and about some by then and I sat under a tree with Jenny, and we talked about the old times back in Indiana when she was just a ragtag tomboy kid and I was one of the current tribe of woods hellions. We talked about friends and families and how the world was and how it had seemed then. We went way back, and I recalled there had been times I had thought about her some, even then.

But then there was the time she was gone, off with kinfolks in the Ohio Valley, and that had been most of three years. When she showed up again around Burnham she wasn't the same old little Jenny. She wasn't a Jenny I knew anymore. But by then the hard times had set in and there wasn't any chance for me to backtrack and get to know her over again. So she just sort of stayed the little Jenny I knew.

"And am I still?" she asked now.

"Some ways you are. But a whole lot more, too. You've grown up, Jenny, and it took me a while to notice."

"I'm glad you notice now." She was quiet for a while, then she asked, "What now, Jeremy?"

"We still have a ways to go before these folks can get settled. I guess you've come this far, and so have I. We might as well go the rest of the way." The air was mild with spring and alive with birdsong, and for the first time in a week or more I wasn't hurting very much. I leaned back against the tree and closed my eyes. "You said you wanted to go west with me."

"You never said I could."

"That never stopped you."

Across the way Hazen Burnett was squiring Eleanor Puckett around, and when they thought nobody was watching they held hands. "Look at them," I said, feeling very drowsy again. "It's spring and the sap is flowing."

"Yes," Jenny said. "It certainly is. Tell me where we'll go, Jeremy, and how it will be."

"Be quiet. I want to listen to the sunlight."

Later, when I was in control of my faculties, it gnawed at me that I had left a matter unresolved, that I hadn't explained something that needed explaining, and that if I wasn't very careful I was going to hurt the girl who saved my life.

But there wasn't much time for talking for a

while after that. With first morning light we lined out southwest, putting as much of Missouri behind us each day as the wagons could cover. We came on a fine day to Excelsior Springs where we stocked up on supplies, got our smithing done, and then headed for Westport.

When this group had formed in Springfield, and later when it left civilization at Hannibal, it had been forty-four overland wagons, three supply wagons, a surrey, and various separate humans and stock. It was more than that now. It had fought and bled and forged itself into a community. These had been just people. Now they were a people. What rolled into Westport on the ninth of April was a town on wheels, and we rolled high and proud as we came in.

A hundred miles of wilderness had perfected our phalanx order, and that was the way Chapman brought us in. We were a sight to behold. We rolled into town and went straight down Market Street to the river road, then turned south in columns of threes toward the staging grounds out on the bluffs. It was midday and the townsfolk turned out to watch the parade. There was Billy Hawk out front, an elegant savage on a prancing steel-dust pony, Mason Chapman up on a black, then Jed O'Hannon's tall wagon with Hazen Burnett and me flanking it, Hazen on his favorite bay and me on the Morgan. Following us were the Simms family, Roy Jenkins and Pat Wall and his tribe in the first column, the Morton wagon with Jenny driving, the Haliburtons and the Blakes next, and so on.

A platoon of uniformed cavalry with nothing better to do fell in fore and aft to escort us to the staging ground, ignoring a few grumbles about where were they back when we needed them, and all we needed to complete the picture was a band. Mr. Tetherstall was no band, but he did blow "Sweet Molly's Drawers" a time or two. This early in the year, we were the best entertainment Westport had seen.

There were other wagons at the staging grounds, small groups from all over waiting to join parties heading west, and some of them might join us. For most of them this was the beginning of a trip overland. There were four families aiming for the middle Platte, and three trying to make up a group to go all the way to the Rocky Mountains. There were standoffish Mormons bound for Brigham Young's valley, Mennonites for the flint hills, and Lutherans for the settlement at Marysville. And there was one cluster of squabbling Methodists who had changed their minds and now intended to head back the way we had come and build themselves a town on the Grand River.

When we rolled in, forty-five wagons and one surrey strong, our columns peeled off right and left and formed a big circle right in the middle of the grounds. Then Jed O'Hannon called a meeting.

From here to the Neosho was ten days with good weather. But that was all patented land out there and we were sure we had no claim to it. Maybe some of it could be bought from those who held it, maybe not. Beyond was wild country and not much known about it except what trail went where. The Santa Fe Trail cut through that country, but it was a big, wide-open land and few lived out there except the Indians.

Farmers need settlements. The hunter can go his way alone, but farmers find their strength in numbers. Bringing in a crop is full-time work, and place-rooted. Farmsteads need to cluster, to defend one another, to trade and grow and thrive.

"I would see the Neosho," O'Hannon told them. "But if we can't stop there, there are no settlements beyond."

Pat Wall rose to his feet, a tall man with a beard the color of rust. "Then what do you call this, Jed?" He swept an arm toward the circle of wagons. "If we are together, where we light will be a settlement, and stronger than some I have seen."

"There is land," Asa added. "Maybe it isn't where we thought, but there is land out there to farm."

The talk went around the circle, talk of places and possibilities, and it was good, serious discussion. Finally Jed told them, "We can rest here a while, and all think about it, then we'll meet again and decide."

Mason Chapman stood. "I contracted to take these wagons to the Neosho, and it sounds like that is your . . . ah . . ."

"Tentative decision," I said.

"Right. Well, I'll take you there, and beyond if you want. When you firm up your tenta . . . ten . . . your plan, we'll settle on route and rolling order. There may be some here who will want to join us."

Hazen Burnett was standing next to me and his eyes never left Eleanor Puckett across the way. "I concur," he muttered, "with the tentative decision."

Our first day at the staging grounds Artemis Steen headed back into Westport to purge his pockets of paper and put a lot more garbage in the newspapers. That day and the next a lot of us spent a lot of time riding back and forth to testify before a court of inquiry regarding the events at Camden Road Cut. I wasn't up to heavy hauling yet, so I spent the most time there, doing my bit to maintain officialdom's required level of confusion. It bothered me that I had serious things to discuss with Jenny, so she and I wouldn't get off on a dangerous tangent, but there just wasn't any time right then to get a discussion going.

The third day there, Hazen Burnett rode into town and brought back a preacher.

There was a grand to-do at the staging grounds that day. The women went into that frenzy that grips women before a wedding. The men did as they were told and stayed out of the way as best they could. Eleanor was everywhere, demure and pretty and running things with an iron hand, and poor Hazen was confused and bewildered and I found that I was very happy for him. Much more so than for me.

I was sitting on the tongue of Jacob Purvis's wagon, regretting some things I had said back there on the trail, and some things I hadn't said yet, when Jenny appeared from somewhere and sat beside me.

"Don't they look happy?" she said, and it was said in that way women have of saying a thing when what they are saying isn't really what they are saying at all.

I knew what it was about. And I should have already had matters set straight before now, because now I couldn't think how to do it. I didn't know what to say so I didn't say anything.

Then she said, in a small voice, "Jeremy?"

"I don't think he looks all that happy," I said.

Then she didn't say anything for a while. Then I felt her hand on my arm and she said again, "Jeremy?" When I turned to her I was looking into eyes so big I could have drowned in them. I had to turn away to keep from falling in.

"Jenny, I guess I said some things back there I shouldn't have. I meant them, every one, but . . . well, right now I can't . . . maybe sometime, but . . ."

"Jeremy Burke," she said with tears in her eyes, "you are impossible!" She stormed away, and I felt like I had stomped on a kitten.

Grace O'Hannon, Anne Morton, and Mrs. Simms came hunting me. Grace put her hands on her hips and thrust out a belligerent chin. "Jeremy Burke, you ought to be ashamed of yourself."

I agreed, and I was, and no sense debating it. So I explained.

"I just don't have any choice," I told them. "I have fourteen dollars and a good Morgan horse, and that's all I have to my name. I don't have anything to offer a wife."

"You'll have a hundred dollars when we get to the Neosho," Grace said. "Jed told me. And a hundred more if you stay on with us where we settle."

"Mr. Burnett is taking himself a wife," Mrs. Simms said, as though that were my fault.

"And they'll have something to start a life on," I told her. "Hazen will have his pay, the same as me, and that will put a crop in the ground. And he's marrying into a family. They'll have their wagon and their gear and the means to start a homestead. They can manage from there. That gives Hazen a base to start from. However it comes, a man has to have that or he's not suited to marry."

Anne Morton was looking at me in that wise, all-knowing way that only women seem to have. She nodded. "I thought it might be some fool thing like that." She walked past me to the chuck box and set a wrapped bundle on it. "Look here, Jeremy Burke. I want to show you something."

She unwrapped it. Inside was a collection of things of value: a stack of currency tied in a ribbon, a little bag of gold and silver coins, a beautiful gold pocket watch, a ruby pin, and some rings, things like that. It was a sizable little treasure.

"These are Jenny's things," she said. "She has been saving them since she was a little girl, waiting for the day you would ask her to marry you. Everything she has ever owned is right here, and when she set out to find you she brought it all with her. There's your start, Jeremy Burke. That girl has been gathering a stake in life for you since she was old enough to set her mind."

I know I went white around the jaws then as the whole thing struck me. Jenny Sutton had ridden across part of Indiana and half of Illinois, alone in the winter, and then trailed through the wildest lands east of Westport, to offer me all in the world she had ever had—a treasure for me because I would need a treasure when I got wherever I was going. And the real treasure she had kept for me was herself.

I hadn't cried but once since I was nine years old, but now I was blinking at moisture that hadn't been there before.

"This is Jenny's dowry," Anne Morton said. "Now you take this and you get yourself over there and you do the decent thing."

I got myself over there and did.

"Somebody wants to see you, Jeremy!" The voice was one of many in a haze of activity and frantic hustling. "Yonder by the river."

CHAPTER NINETEEN

In these hours toward evening of the day the preacher came, I was doing a lot of hurrying around and feeling numb, but no serious thinking. It doesn't pay a man to think on his wedding day. I had got shaved and boot-blacked, had my hair slicked and a borrowed collar half choking me, and when they said go to the river it was just another shove in a bunch of shoves, so I walked down to the river. And there below the floodbank, on a willow-shaded bar, I walked bedazzled through the brush and out into the open square in front of two belted horsemen.

They sat their saddles, just staring at me, and the shock was like cold water on my senses. The one on the left, hunched atop a low-slung bay, was Mark Hayden, his face twisted and bandaged, his eyes alive with a fire like that Bethune, the Sand Creek killer. He stared at me. His hand was at his belt gun and his eyes were red and ugly. Beside him and a little behind, cold and distant atop his tall black, was Sonny Sutton.

I must have gaped at him. Then I said, "Sonny?"

"Found this'n back a ways, Jeremy. He brought me to you."

"Burke!" Hayden's voice was cracked with hatred. "You. You did it. You spoiled it all, Burke. But never again!"

He already had his gun half out of the holster,

and now he heaved it out.

But I guess nobody ever told him that a gun draws best from a hand-down position. It just comes faster to slap leather than to pull from it. My pa knew that. And I had always known it.

The big old Walker spoke, and in its recoil I felt Hayden's shot tug at my sleeve. Hayden stiffened atop his horse, and his mouth opened. But the hole in him was dead center and he was dead. The gun slipped from his fingers and he followed it to the ground. I shifted to cover Sonny, but he hadn't moved. He just sat there, cool and distant, his hands clear.

"You always were a hand with that, Jeremy. Is Jenny all right?"

"She's just fine, Sonny. Come see for yourself."

So Jenny had family at the wedding. Sonny sat his black horse back beyond the crowd, a long white coat flared out around him, a black hat shading those strange, light eyes that didn't miss a thing.

Afterward I went to him with Jenny at my side, and I stood tall and proud and looked up at him. "Is there something you want of me, Abraham?"

"If there was," he said after a moment, "it doesn't count now."

Funny thing . . . it turned out he had been down to St. Louis and had struck up a partnership with another fellow there. They had cleaned up, selling shares in a mining venture on the Mississippi, then had cashed in and gone looking for bigger things. Sonny was due to meet his partner down at Nacogdoches, Texas, in a month or so, and they were going west from there. They had heard about a river over in the Comanche country that had purple pearls growing in it.

Forty-nine wagons, three supply wagons, and a

surrey rolled out of Westport two days later, bound west, maybe for the Neosho, maybe somewhere else, and it didn't really matter. There would be a place, and when we found that place we would stop and build, and put down roots for our children to grow from.

And I knew that among them, with each generation, would be some with an itch in their feet and a far-off look in their eyes, and it would be for them to pick up from where we put down. It would be their turn then to know the westering.

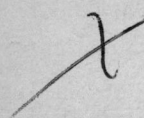

FORGE AHEAD IN THE SCOUT SERIES
BY BUCK GENTRY

#10: TRAITOR'S GOLD (1209, $2.50)
There's a luscious red-head who's looking for someone to lead her through the Black Hills of the Dakotas. And one look at the Scout tells her she's found her man—for whatever job she has in mind!

#11: YAQUI TERROR (1222, $2.50)
The Scout's rescue of a lovely and willing young lady leads him into the midst of a revolution. Even with battles raging around him, Eli proves to her once again that a hard man is good to find!

#12: YELLOWSTONE KILL (1254, $2.50)
The Scout is tracking a warband that kidnapped some young and lovely ladies. And there's danger at every bend in the trail as Holten closes in, but the thought of all those women keeps the Scout riding hard!

#13: OGLALA OUTBREAK (1287, $2.50)
When the Scout's long time friend, an Oglala chief, is murdered, Holten vows to avenge his death. But there's a young squaw who's appreciation for what he's trying to do leads him down an exciting trail of her own!

#14: CATHOUSE CANYON (1345, $2.50)
Enlisting the aid of his Oglala friends, the Scout plans to blast a band of rampaging outlaws to hell—and hopes to find a little bit of heaven in the arms of his sumptuous companion . . .

#15: TEXAS TEASE (1392, $2.50)
Aiding the Texas Rangers, with the luscious Louise on one side and the warring Kiowa-Apache on the other, Eli's apt to find himself coming and going at exactly the same time!

Available wherever paperbacks are sold, or order direct from the Publisher. Send cover price plus 50¢ per copy for mailing and handling to Zebra Books, 475 Park Avenue South, New York, N.Y. 10016. DO NOT SEND CASH.